# LIFETIME

# Scott Sommer

# LIFETIME

RANDOM HOUSE  NEW YORK

Copyright © 1978, 1981 by Scott Sommer

All rights reserved under International and Pan-American Copyright
Conventions. Published in the United States by Random House, Inc.,
New York, and simultaneously in Canada by
Random House of Canada Limited, Toronto.

Library of Congress Cataloging in Publication Data

Sommer, Scott.
Lifetime.

I. Title.
PS3569.06533L5    813'.54    80–6017
ISBN 0–394–51465–3

"Waiting for Merna" was previously published in *Epoch,*
in slightly different form.

A portion of "Crisscross" was previously
published in *Penthouse.*

*Manufactured in the United States of America*

2 4 6 8 9 7 5 3

FIRST EDITION

*For*
*Judith and Joslyn;*
*the terriers, Harrigan and Lucy;*
*and Wesley Strick*

The argument at bedrock:
I don't want to live on earth
but I want to live.
—JIM HARRISON

# CONTENTS

# WAITING
# FOR
# MERNA

## I AM WAITING

for Merna. I am playing cards with Keith and Dolores and Morris, and Merna has been gone since Armed Forces Day, nine days ago. She is in Hawaii. I am on this patio, in this complex, at Arcadian Acres in Atlanta. Today is Memorial Day. The pool opened two hours ago, and ever since, the screams and splashes of children have been heard in the wind. Today the wind is warm and smells of chlorine.

The pool is on the other side, the street side of this particular row of apartments, which is six units long and two units high and constructed of cheap red brick, which chips easily and dissolves to clay in this season's heavy Georgia rains.

## MERNA

is a stewardess on Flight 434 Atlanta to San Francisco to Hawaii. I suspect her of having an affair with the copilot of this flight. Suspicion is more discomforting than verification, and the last few evenings I have been awakened by terrible dreams of envy. In these dreams I disrobe Merna before a panel of judges. I discover sand in her panties. The judges find this evidence amusing.

## MORRIS AND KEITH AND I

sit shirtless in short pants. Sun is above us. It is noon. Wind stirs the lilacs, but we do not smell them today. Today the wind is chlorine. Today Merna is flying home to me. Dolores wears a blue halter top that resembles Merna's blue halter top, but Dolores does not remind me of Merna. The four of us have been drinking wine. Intermittently, Keith has suggested that Dolores remove her blue top, which has become stained with perspiration. Morris laughs at this suggestion. The laugh impresses me as a bad parody of villainous prurience.

## MORRIS

suffered a heart attack this past autumn and is recuperating here at Arcadian Acres. At present, like myself, he is officially unemployed (although, as I learned two days ago, this is not the actual situation). Recently the management has grown impatient with the tardiness with which Morris pays his monthly rental bill and is threatening him with eviction. What's more, residents from adjacent apartment rows are trying to evict him on the grounds that he allows his Doberman pinscher to run free on the complex in violation of the *Arcadian Acres Agreements*, which we all pledged to uphold. Morris is amused by these threats. In fact, he seems to savor them for the dramatic lift they provide. "Don't you kid yourself," he has told me in haughty Brooklynese. "They know my reputation. They would not dare!"

I, however, do not know of Morris's reputation. He tells me very little. He tells me he is forty-five and a former Golden Gloves champion from Sheepshead Bay, Brooklyn. But this is all he tells me.

There are two bare circles amid the hair on Morris's pectoral muscles where, not long ago, cardiograph instruments had been pasted. The hair on his head is not dissimilar to this chest hair; it is wiry and brown and short, and the beard he has grown this past month is of the same texture and length but is made more interesting by bright orange highlights.

Morris's eyes sparkle with an irony that suggests, simultaneously, innocence and ruthlessness, anger and affection. Though I feel a helpless affection and regard for him, I am wary of his every move. I am nearly convinced he is in the process of conning Merna and me and the others, but I do not know to what end. Last March, for instance, when I caught him on the patio taking a clipping from Dolores's spider plant, he whispered, "Trust me, sweetheart; but be suspicious!"

Morris jogs every morning to a YMCA where he exercises for two hours with other members of the Northeast Atlanta Heart Attack Club. Morris is divorced and drives a '67 Squire wagon with New York license plates. This divorce business I learned from Keith.

KEITH,

too, is divorced. His former wife found him in bed with Dolores. Keith is thirty and a musician at a glass downtown hotel which features a translucent elevator that ascends and descends along the exterior of the structure. Dolores is a waitress there. The two of them work nights and live above Merna and me. At dawn we hear their bed creak and rock. They are both alcoholics, and the other day, the fifth day of Merna's absence, Keith drunkenly confided to me that Dolores drinks too much and often quits on him in bed. He inquired if I was the type interested in "trading off" partners. I told him that indeed, I was not the type, and against my better judgment I was polite about it. (Since my suspicion of Merna began, I am losing my sense of humor about infidelity.)

KEITH'S TWO-YEAR-OLD SON,

Jack, lives in Minnesota now with his mother, who works for a grain company in St. Paul. Whenever I see Keith sitting alone in the late afternoon sunlight, sipping milk with Brewer's yeast, I assume he is thinking of how it felt to hold his little son, Jack.

I recall glancing through the breakfast window last January

to see him standing with his former wife and son in the macadam lot. It was snowing softly. The boy was trying to catch the flakes. "Say goodbye to your father," his mother told him. "Say bye-bye." Keith stood in an undershirt. His back was to me and there was a roll of fat at his hips. He kissed the boy softly on the cheek and walked up the stairs. The wife tossed the boy in the car and stood staring up at Keith. From the window I could see Keith's shoes and bare ankles on the metal stairway. "I'll make you sorry, you bastard," she told him. "Drive carefully," Keith replied. I listened to him climb the remaining stairs and then heard a door close. His wife spotted me at the little window. She was blinking furiously. "You go to hell!" she cried.

I SIT OPPOSITE DOLORES

and Morris on a wooden picnic table which Arcadian Acres intends the ground-floor and second-floor tenants to share. The sun is directly above us; it is on my shoulders. Keith is to my right. He is telling a story about a gig in Mobile. Whenever he laughs I smell digesting wine. He is drunk and his words slur. It is noon. Birds drift in the easterly wind that smells of chlorine today and is hurrying Merna home to me.

I feel something between my legs. I look abashedly to Dolores, but her eyes are glazed and lifeless and staring elsewhere. I discover Morris, a moment later, grinning boyishly. He winks and nods his head toward Dolores. "You wish!" he says. The wine, no doubt, has gotten the better of him. "Take it easy on the juice," I suggest. "Who are you?" he replies. "My mother?" This evokes laughter from Dolores, but she does not lift her head from the cards. She is not an intelligent woman, and her alcoholic reticence exacerbates this impression of dullness. Whenever she does speak, she is drunk to the point of incoherence and waxes endlessly about the miracle of her contact lenses. At present, she says to Morris, "You crack me up, mister!" To which Keith appends, "Don't give him the chance!" Morris is offended by this and points an admonishing finger at Keith. "Watch out now!" he says. When I smile, he adds angrily, "That means everybody!"

Only once before have I seen Morris react with such vehemence. I had asked him a direct question concerning his past. "Who are you?" he replied. "A detective?"

KEITH AND DOLORES

are far less secretive than Morris, but they are less interesting citizens, and so I am disinclined to ask them questions. Frankly, I find them a bit depressing, and the more I know of them the more estranged I feel from them. (At best, friendship in this city of sun-belt transients is a tenuous business; it is founded on future aspirations, not the past, which everyone, apparently, has come here to forget.)

ACROSS THE LOT

there is a row of apartments six units long and two units high, and it is identical in color and construction to the one in which Dolores and Keith and Morris and Merna and I live. Though I am unfamiliar with all the citizens who inhabit the twelve apartments, I know that opposite our apartment there lives a Mexican family, the Ortegas, who have grown a garden in the six- by four-foot patch of land each lessee is entitled to call his own. Mr. Ortega is growing tomatoes and Mrs. Ortega corn, and they always work in the garden at different times; in fact, it appears as if they have consciously scheduled it this way.

MR. ORTEGA

is unemployed these days and leaves the complex at seven every morning with the intention of finding a position on a man-power construction crew. A local firm has been demolishing a three-block area downtown, and each evening they advertise "Workers Wanted" in the *Constitution*. Mr. Ortega, however, is home every morning at eight-thirty, complaining of discrimination. Mrs. Ortega is impatient with this explanation by now, and last week the two of them began screaming at each other in the parking lot. She believes (according to Jorge Marguez, their neighbor) that he has been driving around town, eyeballing the women. So recently Mrs. Ortega placed an advertisement in the *Arcadian Acres Announcements*, which is distributed weekly on stiff green paper to the more than two hundred lessees in the complex, informing us, among other things, of recent marriages, births, new tenants, job promotions, furniture sales, and lost pets. Last week, under "Arcadian Services," Mrs. Ortega wrote that she would be available for babysitting and domestic work at reasonable prices. Jorge Marguez believes she is trying to embarrass her husband into work. Three days ago, for ten dollars, Morris hired Mrs. Ortega to clean his entire apartment.

MRS. ORTEGA AND HER DAUGHTER

drink coffee in the early spring sunlight after Mr. Ortega leaves at seven in his maroon Duster. I watch them from my patio, sipping coffee by myself. Frequently the daughter's boyfriend, who lives in the apartment directly above the Ortegas, joins the women before leaving for work. The boyfriend stocks canned goods at the local A&P. I have seen him there on one or two occasions, reorganizing cans of vegetables and muttering to himself, but we have never acknowledged each other's existence with anything like a simple wave of hand or nod of head. (Keith tells me he carries a loaded pistol in the trunk of his VW, and perhaps for this reason I want nothing to do with him.) He is gone by seven forty-five, driving the daughter to the nearby vocational school, where she studies typing and shorthand, and it is at this time that Mrs. Ortega commences her daily weeding and hoeing in the garden. She stops when Mr. Ortega pulls up in his Duster, a weary and angry look on his face. She retreats indoors, not to be seen until the following morning. (It is possible, of course, that she sits in the shade on the other side of her apartment. I, however, have never gone to look, as it depresses me to wander around Arcadian Acres.)

ONE OF MR. ORTEGA'S LEGS IS SLIGHTLY SHORTER

than the other, and on one shoe there is affixed a large corrective heel. Nevertheless, he walks with a slight rocking motion, which reminds Dolores of a duck waddle and makes her snicker nastily. Mr. Ortega is a diminutive man who wears heavy black-rimmed glasses, which seem to shrink his small head even further and exaggerate his disproportionately large ears. He removes these glasses while sitting in the sun, eyes closed, until shadows surround him. Then he rises to begin working his hour in the garden. By the time he has finished, Dolores and Keith have awakened to play hearts with Morris and me. In the afternoon, after his lunch, while we play cards, Mr. Ortega polishes the Duster from hood to trunk. Afterward he vacuums the interior carefully before jacking up the entire body to examine the exhaust system. At least twice a week Mr. Ortega rotates the tires and inspects the brake drums for leaks. At the moment, he is changing the oil. He is well beneath the car, and I am nervous that the jack might kick out and leave him pinned. I do not, however, communicate this anxiety to anyone, particularly to Mr. Ortega, who I feel wants to be left alone these difficult recession days. (This is not to suggest that Mr. Ortega is unsociable. He has numerous companions and seems quite animated and joyful in their presence.)

JORGE MARGUEZ,

for example, lives on the eastern extreme of the same apartment row as Mr. Ortega, and ever since Jorge returned from the hospital after a hernia operation, the two of them have spent most of the late afternoon and early evening talking excitedly in Spanish about one thing or another.

Jorge came from Cuba immediately after the revolution and is somewhat embittered about the confiscation of his father's shoe factory. These days he loads crates at the nearby Sears Automotive Center during the day and works another eight-hour evening shift as a floor manager at Beef House, where he injured himself moving the drink machine. Once when I politely attempted to argue the merits of the revolution, Jorge grew livid with me. "We are talking here about fascism," he protested. "Either the left-handed dictator or the right-handed one. Both they are the same: both bastards!"

Jorge is a bachelor who devotes a great deal of time to the singles bars in the more suburban sectors of Atlanta. Although he delights in relating his social escapades, he is a Catholic who does not believe in premarital relations; hence there is something wildly incongruous about his narrations. He will elaborate, for instance, on so-and-so's breasts and so-and-so's ass, but at the same time he will talk of marrying so-and-so and raising a family. Since Thanksgiving he has proposed seven times to seven different women, and recently he asked me to translate for him the precise meanings of "creep" and "naïve." I told him, perhaps wrongly, that the words are complimentary, meaning, respectively, "one who is patient and reliable" and "one who is innocent and pure." Afterward, he gazed at me roguishly and I, in turn, winked at him. "They will be corrected after I nail them!" he assured me.

At the moment, he is limping over in his bathrobe and slippers to converse with Mr. Ortega. Jorge is under doctor's orders to relax for five weeks, and he is being a hypochondriac about his postoperative aches and pains. Mr. Ortega has returned to his patio and is preparing an aluminum-framed chair for Jorge, who, in turn, is preparing to show Mr. Ortega his hernia scar for the seventh consecutive day. Smiling, Jorge points to something in Mr. Ortega's garden. The two of them break into giddy laughter, punching each other playfully in the shoulder.

I HAVE BEEN IN ATLANTA SINCE NEW YEAR'S DAY.

I came here to be with Merna, who I suspect is betraying me in Hawaii. My suspicion, I realize, is founded partially upon my own paranoia, but this inclination is aggravated by the nature of my first encounter with Merna, which took place New Year's Eve in Newark's International Airport. We sat in the lounge of The Executive Bar. Across from us, emblazoned in holiday silver, hung the words "The Executive Bar—The Trysting Place for Transients."

Later, in a Holiday Inn suite, we watched the ball descend in Times Square. Outside, trucks and automobiles skidded out of control on the New Jersey Turnpike.

In the morning I watched the silvery ice melt on the window. The cold sun transmuted the ice to an opaque glittering membrane, and everything beyond the pane moved vaguely and insubstantially as shadows. I could hear footsteps on the ceiling and muffled voices through the walls. Merna woke and approached me sleepily. She was naked and hung over; runny mascara formed dark crescents beneath her eyes. On my lap, she asked, "What are your plans?"

"I'm in between things," I said.

"What things?"

"Past and future."

She yawned. The sun burned through the ice and made me squint.

"What about you?" I asked. "What are your plans?"

"My flight leaves at two."

I have been in Arcadian Acres ever since. I am collecting unemployment and food stamps. I am still in between things. Today is Friday. I am playing cards with Keith and Dolores and Morris, and I am waiting patiently for Merna to return from Hawaii (where she has been, so she tells me, temporarily restationed).

I have been aspiring the last three hands to win the game of hearts by "shooting the moon," a risky maneuver which demands the collection of all thirteen hearts and the queen of spades. If I could accomplish this trick, then Keith and Dolores and Morris would be eliminated from the game and I could fall asleep in the sun. I have, however, failed three consecutive times, and it is now probable that I shall lose.

### MY FAILURES

have improved Morris's sense of humor, which, I submit, is unconventional. Each Sunday, for example, he chauffeurs his Doberman to the city park, where he allows the dog to run free and terrorize innocent strollers. In recounting the more brutal of these episodes, such as the time the dog terrified a black child into a tree, Morris laughs with satanic sparks in his eyes. He cherishes these events and retells them throughout the week, during which time they undergo ridiculous permutations, so that by the following Saturday Morris is telling Mrs. Ortega and her daughter that the Doberman treed an alcoholic disrupting a group of picnicking blind women. When I inquire why Morris exaggerates so, he shoots back, "I give people what they want—a good story. Who are you, Mr. Sunday School?"

### MORRIS IS AN OBSTINATE MAN

and it is best not to challenge or contradict him. Just last month Merna asked him for some paprika. When he handed her red pepper instead, she replied that she must have paprika. "What's the matter?" Morris asked incredulously. "Didn't Mother teach you the who's who of the kitchen? Didn't she explain red pepper and paprika is the same garnishment?" He then glanced at her with a condescending smile, as if he was amused by her ignorance.

Morris is also a shameless man, and once Merna had established a precedent of neighborliness, he did not hesitate to requite the gesture. Nowadays, morning or night, Morris will appear at the door wrapped in a towel, dripping wet from a shower, to ask for a little of this or that. It is usually sugar or coffee or milk, and Merna and I are always more than happy to accommodate him. Perhaps it is because he has been divorced and has survived a coronary, all in one year, that we feel this obligation; nonetheless, I am a little disappointed that Merna and I apparently need an excuse or justification for our neighborliness. But in his own calculated way, Morris is touched by our overtures, and not long ago he refunded us with a coffee can filled with bacon fat. "You cook with this," he explained to Merna. "Makes your hair healthful." Then he requested two eggs.

LAST MONTH,
Morris's sixth month of recovery, after we learned he was permitted to drink in moderation, Merna and I purchased a bottle of Wild Turkey bourbon for him, as a gift. After Morris opened the box, which we had carefully wrapped in newspaper, he looked at us and said, unabashedly, "What's the problem with you two? You don't hand a person one gift bottle of booze. Booze gifts come in twos!" The following morning we found at our doorstep the tiny cuttings of a spider plant and a Swedish ivy. The clay pots were tied in red ribbon and Morris had placed the empty bourbon bottle between them.

Morris is inordinately proud of the small collection of plants he has cultivated since his coronary, and every morning, before he jogs to the YMCA to meet with the Heart Attack Club, he rearranges and waters them carefully. Afterward, he will knock at our door with a watering can to ask for toothpaste or a cup of coffee. He will feel obliged to talk with us for a moment, and more times than not he will point to the white circles on his chest and say, "If this hair ain't in by Labor Day, somebody's got a malpractice suit!" Lately, he has taken to pointing at the bare spots and winking at me: "Be nice, bum. You got ten percent." Other times, when he seems to have nothing to relate, he will invite me to his patio to examine a new plant he has purchased, and at such times he surprises me with his knowledge of horticulture.

"But don't you kid yourself," he once told me. "I could take these plants and put them up against anybody's, one on one!" He reinforced these words by pointing his finger emphatically at my chest, as if to intimidate me into agreement. "Shit," he said, "I could make a living selling these weeds. What's so funny with you?"

## THE FAMILY

that lives above Morris consists, or did consist until last month, of an elderly woman and her nephew, a large Neanderthal-looking boy of fourteen. The boy moved in with the aunt two days after I arrived at Arcadian Acres, and immediately thereafter the aunt enrolled him in a special school for students with learning disabilities. The boy's parents, who live in Mobile, apparently bequeathed the boy to the care of the aunt for financial reasons. They came to visit twice a month. I noticed an unusual resemblance between the father and the boy: both had unevenly receding hairlines, which made their heads appear to be awkwardly canted on their necks, and both squinted whenever addressed.

The nephew rode a bus to and from his special school. Generally, I would be returning from a long walk when the bus stopped on the shoulder of the road fronting Arcadian Acres. One rainy afternoon, I saw the nephew alight from the bus with an umbrella. He seemed disturbed about something. From where I stood across the street, I could see he was grumbling to himself when, shielded by the umbrella, he stepped carelessly into the road and was struck by a red truck carrying gravel.

THAT SAME AFTERNOON

(unknown to me at the time) Morris signed a lease for an old gasoline station that he intended to convert into a plant store. This was in April. It rained frequently and ruined Mr. Ortega's tomato plants. Keith and Dolores and Morris and I did not see one another with any regularity. Merna was forced to spend weekends in San Francisco. I felt ambitious and sold flowers on street corners in the afternoons. I missed the hearts I am playing at present (though when I am playing it I find it mildly boring) and I missed talking with Morris. He was gone from early morning until dinner. This went on for nearly a month.

He did not tell anyone of the plant store until two days ago, at which time he presented us with gold-colored invitations to the opening of the House of Father Nature. (To say, then, that Morris is unemployed is obviously inaccurate. Yet by incorporating the store in the names of Germaine—his paramour—and her daughter, Morris has arranged to continue collecting unemployment compensation.)

GERMAINE

is a tall gray-haired woman who operates a wholesale greenhouse in the southern sector of the city. She seems older than Morris and something of a gypsy. She wears her hair in a tight ponytail, and whenever I see her she is dressed in iridescent pants and a multicolored cape. She has mentioned to me that Morris will be working at the store six days a week, but only from three to six in the afternoon. She or her daughter will work the remainder of the day. Frankly, I wonder if an ulterior motive or two does not inform Morris's relationship with her.

YESTERDAY,

when I visited the House of Father Nature, I saw Morris walking with Germaine from customer to customer in dungarees and a yellow straw hat. When we shook hands, he said, "Where the hell have you been? The invitations said three!" It was nearly five. The sun was at my back, making Morris squint. "What's the matter with you?" he said. "Were you bred by a barn?" Then he walked off, telling me to stay put. When he returned, he was carrying a luxuriant fern in his muscular arms. "This is for you," he said gruffly. "My best plant. Don't screw it up!"

I HAVE BEEN PLAYING

cards with Keith and Dolores and Morris. Moments ago I ended the game by throwing a five of hearts and unexpectedly drawing out the two, three, and four of the same suit. This makes Morris laugh and gives me one hundred points. I have lost. I have been left to myself by Merna, who is late (and probably not coming back today as scheduled). I expect a telegram any moment.

"Do you believe," Merna asked me last month, "that you can respect someone as much as you desire them?"

"I hope so," I said.

It was evening. The stars were unusually bright. We were drinking on the patio.

"Desire seems so easy in comparison," she said.

"Well, respecting someone as much as you desire them isn't nearly so hard as walking on water."

Merna looked at me. "If that were to happen to us," she whispered, "what would we do then?"

"Then we would try to live together in the world."

"Strange," she said, "how we can't seem to do that by ourselves."

"No," I said, "by ourselves we can only live in our separate heads."

MORRIS IS LEAVING NOW.

He is returning to his apartment, where he will untie the Doberman, who is chained at the door in the sun, and allow him to terrorize the complex for twenty minutes. Then Morris will shower, change to dungarees and the yellow straw hat, and drive away with the dog in the '67 Squire wagon, which once transported his family along Flatbush Avenue in Brooklyn. He will have trouble starting the car. He will open the hood and punch the battery and thereafter the motor will start cleanly. He will smile and wave to me, shouting something like "It's your type that's wrong with life!" And though he is teasing, I know he believes, as I believe, that he has got something there.

KEITH AND DOLORES STAND BEFORE ME

now at the opposite side of the wooden table. They are drunk. They are beginning to paw affectionately at each other while they perform the customary stretching and yawning exercises that inform their peculiar foreplay. There is a salacious glint in Keith's eye and a gelid, lifeless haze emanating from Dolores's. Before long they will trot up the stairs with surprising spark, and shortly thereafter I will hear a television game show issuing from their bedroom window. They will reappear hours later, at five, each dressed for work—Keith in black tuxedo, Dolores in black leotards, silver panties and blouse. They will sip milk with Brewer's yeast on their upstairs porch, and their subsequent gestures will appear more coherent, their eyes more lucid. They will drive off in Keith's Triumph, leaving behind a whiff of death.

SO I AM

alone here now, my eyes closed to the diminishing sun, which blesses Arcadian Acres. It is Memorial Day and the cries and splashes of exuberant children can be heard in the wind that smells of chlorine. Nine days ago it was Armed Forces Day, and since then there has been nothing for me to do but wait for Merna and contemplate the everydayness that is my life. Yet it occurs to me just now, facing west into the sun, into the sky whence Merna should be emerging in a 727, that something significant has evolved between us these past few months. Desire has taken us as far as it can, has kept the muscles of our hearts pulsing with suspense.

"What will you do while I'm gone?" she asked, packing for Hawaii.

"I don't know," I said. "Play cards. Joke with the others."

"May I ask you something?"

"Naturally."

Merna sat on her suitcase to close it.

"Do you trust me?"

"I do," I said.

"Then try to trust the others, too," she said. "It's important for you. This is the only world either of us will ever get."

IT IS NOW CLEAR TO ME

that Merna is correct. This is all there is. In the end, I imagine, we—Merna and I and all the others, such as my friends here at Arcadian Acres, whom I observe, touch, converse with and overhear—will discover either that our cup is indeed full of modest possibilities or, unhappily, that our cup is in fact an empty crock of selfish and lonely and reckless desire without purpose.

How strange that after all these years I should discover that the way back into the world is concretely all around me, has always been right before my blind and prideful eyes.

LYING HERE NOW WITH MY EYES CLOSED, I UNDERSTAND
that the sun is not a solution. It is simply strong white light that warms and comforts me. It is enough. I can remember Morris standing on the patio with me last week, listening as I carried on about this and that, and I can hear him saying abruptly, "What the hell do you think you are—exempt?"

AT PRESENT,
the screaming of tires and the blast of a horn signal from the parking lot. I open my eyes to discover that an Arcadian Acres maintenance truck has backed into a yellow cab. Jorge Marguez, in his bathrobe, and Mr. Ortega, with his hoe, are walking briskly toward the accident. Keith and Dolores are staring from their bedroom window and Morris is standing on the patio, yelling for the Doberman. A swarm of children in dripping bathing suits comes racing around the eastern side of Morris's apartment to investigate the source of the commotion. I stand, as they race past me, to behold Merna stepping from the yellow cab with a lei hanging around her neck. Her face is browned with sun. Her long russet hair, parted in the middle into two even folds, whips wildly in the wind as she approaches. I stand before her anxiously.

"How did you do?" she asks.

"I missed you," I say simply.

Merna lifts the lei from her head and loops it around mine. I can see Morris and all the others congregated around the cab, watching us.

"Now what are you going to do?" Morris calls out.

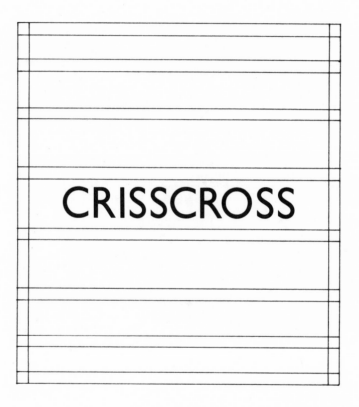

CRISSCROSS

I know that what I did probably looks like very bad news on a roll, but I'm not trying to snap your strap when I say I bet you'd do the same thing if you were ten and your life was as screwed up as mine.

You need to understand Mom to understand me. In '68, which is when I was born, we lived on an Army post in Texas with Dad. When I was two Dad split for 'Nam because Mom said he was a trained killer paid to protect ruling crass interests. When he came back though in '71 he got hip and grew his hair long and wore beads and quit the Army. He started doing yoga and fasting and pretty soon he was taking these two-week vows of silence where he would sit in the tree house he built for me in the backyard and all he'd do was smile and point to stuff around him.

One time we brought his uniform down to the Gulf and started collecting driftwood and made a fire and burned up the complete killer costume. He handed me his captain's hat but I didn't throw it in and I still have it. I got the headband adjusted last year to fit my space capsule, which is what Mom calls my head, and sometimes I wear it when I play frisbee on the beach. It looks pretty strange with long hair, but it's like Mom tells guys who nail her: I'm retarded.

After the uniform had burned up Dad knelt beside me and looked me in the eyes and said, "The meaning of life is to love everything, even flies, you got it?" It was the first thing he had said to me in a month and it was the last thing he said to anyone I know since then because the next day Mom was crying and reading a note to Grandma on the phone and the note said Dad had split for a monastery in New Zealand and wasn't ever coming back. Since then, all I've been thinking about is how come Dad didn't think as much of me and Mom as he did flies?

Mom took me to Key West with her six years ago when she came here to get her head together because my dad's splitting really blew her mind. We were supposed to stay for two weeks, but then Blair came surfsailing along and Mom decided to stay in the sack with him until the buy-centennial. Blair owned a mechanic shop, The Fool's Tool, near the cemetery, and a lot of times back then Mom would leave me with Blair when she went to work at the yogurt stand on Duval Street. Blair would give me money for the pop machine to keep me busy, so all day I drank Coke and sat by the air hose, blowing up balloons until they exploded and counting lizards when they ran from the grass across the parking lot and into the grass again. I always worried somebody would pull in and crush them, but they never did, though sometimes I had to jump in front of cars just to make sure, and Blair would always shout from under a hood, "What the fuck you doin', Coke!" which is how I got my nickname, though now I think most people will start calling me that for other reasons—if you can dig it!

I hardly ever saw Blair get paid with money from a customer because most of the time he swapped with them. They'd come in for their wheels and when they'd ask how much he'd say, "For one g of nose and a source of Percodan we'll entitle it even," because like everybody else on this key he was a drug maniac and needed the stuff to make his heart keep the faith.

One time some guy was real low on bread and dry as a desert in the drug department, so Blair offered to take a puppy from the guy's dog's litter, which is how I got Leon my retarded hundred-pound wolf dog—my best friend next to Buggs and

Emmett, even if all Leon ever does is chase rocks and sleep in front of The House Hotel and sniff Termina's crotch whenever it's real hot, which is all the time. Termina is Bugg's sister and she and me are pretty tight at this point. Termina's eleven but knows how to have orgasms.

Blair abandoned Mom like Dad did, but I didn't care. He just split one day on a sailboat for Cayman Island. I felt bummed for Mom because it flipped her out and made her feel like a two-time loser and she started getting high all the time instead of just at night.

After the rent went sayonara at the end of the month at Blair's pad, Mom and me moved into The House Hotel because Mom was working in the restaurant there, so the room only cost her twenty-five bucks a week. It wasn't too much of a drag at The House sleeping on the floor in a sleeping bag next to Mom's bed and I even got into going down the hall to the bathroom, but one time everybody in The House—minus me because I don't have dick hairs yet—came down with the crabs after some whore from Miami infected the toilet on the second floor.

Emmett the Huge came around and apologized to everyone about the crabs and offered to return their money. Emmett's sixty-six and fat with a big nose and long gray hair, which is cool since he used to be Stanley's barber in Montana before he bought The House with Stanley, who was in 'Nam the same year as Dad and who had his knee screwed up pretty good from a land mine, so now Stanley gets a lot of money from the government for disability which he uses mostly, Mom says, to buy party drugs and uniforms for The House softball team. Emmett is the only straight one in the place because he's thirty years older than anyone else, though he occasionally does up a joint with me on the sun deck or in his house behind The House. Emmett's really a nervous wreck who chain-smokes and has two kids older than Mom. He's been divorced for a long time like everyone else around here and he seems pretty lonesome. I know when he's dreaming of the guillotines because then he plays chess by himself and talks out loud to himself in different voices.

I try not to get too close to Emmett even though I really dig him because the way he chain-smokes at his age I figure he could drop dead like a fly at any second now and it is really a nightmare to dig someone and then have them cut out on you.

Last month Emmett came to school with me after the principal, Sadist Shapiro, had sent me home because he said my hair was too long and that I looked like an animal. I said, "Cool, fool, I ain't comin' back," and stayed away for a week. I went to the beach and played frisbee with Leon and didn't tell anyone. Except that Shapiro wrote Mom a letter and said that if I didn't get my hair cut and my act together and show up for classes the following week that he would try to get me sent to a special school for "emotionally disturbed youths."

I was in my red bathing suit at the beach with the bandanna wrapped around my head when Emmett came and got me. We walked into Sadist's office that afternoon of the letter and found him watching cartoons on TV! Sadist told Emmett I was the worst fourth-grader in history and disrupted Miss Smethurst's class. Emmett wheezed a couple of times and nodded and told Shapiro that he had friends on Key Largo who made a living taking care of people who picked on children. So the next week I showed up for school with cowboy boots and shades and my long hair and Shapiro didn't say a word. But I guess now he'll have the last laugh because I'll probably wind up where he wanted me in the first place: in a cage.

Jetty is the head cook at The House restaurant. He says he's old enough to be my father so I shouldn't wise off to him. He has long brown hair that he braids so he looks like an Indian when he's tan, which is almost always because he's real laid back and digs catching rays. He's always smoking a peace pipe that's

filled with hash and when he's not high he's nasty as a bastard
and gives me nuggies on the head by making one knuckle stick
out on his first. The nuggies really piss off Mom because she
says violence is ghoulish and foolish but Jetty says it's an education in the school of hard knocks, which makes Mom smile at
him like she's going to throw up something green.

Jetty is also the pitcher on The House softball team and also
the coach of the women's softball team where Mom plays right
field because she isn't too cool at high flies since she's so high
herself, and Jetty is even a bastard with the "girls," which is
what he calls them, though all the women tell him to call them
women, but he says, "Fuck you guys. Let's play ball, not ball-
buster, okay!" His team isn't too good and he gets ragged a lot
and starts screaming, "Jesus Christ, Carla, there's a fucking
lefty up! Play the goddamn hole, will you!" Or he'll say to Mom,
"Shit! Hit the cutoff man. You should've had her dead!" When
he's stoned though he's funny and does imitations of animals.
The regulars who eat at The House know you've got to be cool
about hassling Jetty about getting on the stick with your food
because lots of times he just sits down and imitates a sad mon-
key and raps about something with Lewis, the fat dishwasher
from Brooklyn who plays shortstop on the team.

Lewis is the best infielder even though he's wrecked out of
his mind before a game, but that's because he says softball's no
fun if you're straight and that it's great getting off on the game
when you're about ten light-years away in your head. The
Cuban dude, Padillo, the old man without front teeth and a bird
nose who wears short pants and black socks and a weird little
hat really digs the way Lewis plays and he's always shouting,
"E c pway, Yuwey! E c pway!" If Lewis and Jetty get rapping
too much in the kitchen and I'm around then Jetty or Stanley
makes me go around to the tables and tell the guests that the
stove is fucked up and it'll be a few more minutes before the
omelets are done.

• • •

One day is when it started. Jetty asked me if I still had the Zodiac inflatable with the motor mounted that Blair left for me and Mom after he abandoned us. I said to Jetty, "Does Society have its head invested where it smarts?" because that's Jetty's favorite expression, so he said if I wanted three sticks of dyno-weed and an album of my choice, then I should take Zodiac out to his brother Snyder's shrimper, *Tchandee*, which was just south of Curry's Dock, and pick up these special fish he needed for dinner at the restaurant. I felt bad about having something to do with killing fish because of what my dad said about loving everything—even flies!—but I still did what Jetty asked because I wanted him to give me five when I got back and maybe get stoned with me. Also I was real glad to go because it was so nice outside and the last thing I needed was to go back to school after lunch and listen to Smethurst the Worst try to convince us that Society is good for you and that we should all become good business zombies when we grow up and play dead.

So I took Zodiac to *Tchandee* and cut the motor and called up to Snyder and he climbed down the gunwale and tossed me these yellow snappers all locked in at the gills on this long metal hook that made me sick because I could see tears in the fishes' eyes, but I was cool and winked at Snyder and gunned the outboard in reverse and then popped her forward and swung Zodiac around in its own wake and took off back to Curry's Dock. I was scared being so far out and tried not to think about sharks or the loggerhead sea turtles that could eat me in one snap-crackle-pop!

I thought something was a little fishy that night when Mom served me dinner in the restaurant. I was sitting next to Lewis and his flipped-out lover Stephanie, whose mouth is always dirty and who smells a little like Leon. Kelley was across from me. She's only nine years older than me but real sexy and Stanley's lover. Kelley's always got a runny nose that until not too long ago I thought was a cold, but now I'm hip to what Kelley's into and why she laughs a lot and talks real slow and sexy. She was giving Stanley "fuck eyes" as Jetty says, so I figured something was weird that night because everyone's nose sounded like Kelley's nose and Jetty served conch fritters instead of yellow snapper. I was cool though and ate my millet and just asked Jetty what happened to the snapper I got for dinner. Jetty was in a bastard mood and said, "Just eat up and make it snappy, all right!" And Lewis said in his Brooklyn accent and hoarse voice, "Look, punko, you got what you wanted, so pipe down!" Mom got fed up and said, "If you can't speak nicely to my kid, keep your stupid Uranus shut!"

I ate faster than is good for you and also had suspicious thoughts while I was eating, which is really bad for you according to Emmett because it makes good food poisonous. But I was late for work at the stand and had to split. I slipped through the big glassless window that leads onto the patio where there are outdoor eating tables and mounted Bicycle. Mom said, "Watch out for cars!" and I said, "You're the one always in trouble!"

I got stoned on one of the dyno joints Jetty gave me for the fish because business at the stand was bad news and the softball game was worse. People were buying crud instead of the good stuff Emmett and me had ordered, so I just stood behind the counter blowing bubbles from the plastic hoop and watching them float up toward the night lights that looked like UFOs landing all around the field. I watched the bubbles float over the field until they popped and disappeared, like they were gone into another dimension, which is where my dad says God exists.

The thing that got me depressed and made me get stoned that night was that people kept asking for soda and potato chips instead of trying the organic almonds and the organic apple juice I'd ordered after Emmett showed me how to fill in the After the Fall Company order form. Every time somebody said,

"Gimme a pop, Coke," or "Two packs of chips and a frank, Hank!" I said, "Get hip to the apple juice and almonds—they don't cost any more." And they said, "Just gimme the pop and chips and shut up." I told them what Emmett told me about what caffeine and sugar and artificial color and flavoring and salt do to your body, but they didn't want to hear about it because they said it was Friday night and they needed to air out their heads, not do a health number on them.

Emmett told me not to take personally what people bought because he says people have the Sickness unto Death and a Death Wish also, so all I said to people was, "Cool be a fool!" and sold them the crap they wanted. Toward the end of the game though I had so much apple juice and almonds I didn't know where to store it all, so I took a box and put cups of juice in it and I put the almonds in cups also and went around the stands and gave them out to the little kids for free. Pat, the guy who nails Mom when she's too high for her own good, was really drunk as usual and wanted some almonds, but I said they were only for the kids and he said, "I'm still a kid, man!" and I said for kids without hair on their tools, and everyone around him was real stoned and started cracking up like idiots and Stephanie, Lewis's filthy lover, started beeping her bicycle horn and saying, "I'm gawna die, I'm gawna fucking die from that kid!"—meaning me.

Sometimes when I see all these people jumping around in the little green bleachers cheering like lobotomy cases I think I understand why Dad flipped out and went to a monastery instead of wasting his life drinking beer and soda and stumbling around on 'ludes watching dumb softball games. I just wish he'd have been uncrazy enough to know better than to leave without me.

By the last week in October, which seems like much more than a month ago now, I was going almost every day to *Tchandee* and leaving school early by just not going back after lunch. A couple of times Smethurst the Worst sent me to Sadist Shapiro's office the next day to see what gave, and I told Shapiro that Emmett and his friends in Key Largo said it was okay for me to stay away when I didn't feel like letting the school brainwash me. Shapiro turned white and got mad and tried to tell me that Mom and Emmett and everyone else associated with The House were sick degenerate drug addicts, so I told Shapiro that Stanley had lots of weapons still from his 'Nam days and that he'd protect me if Shapiro started acting real big. Shapiro looked scared and called in The Worst and told the old bag to just ignore me because someday I'd get mine and realize how disrespectful and neurotic a person I was. So I told Shapiro that Emmett and me were writing a letter to the State Board of Miseducation to make them hip to the news that Shapiro was watching cartoons on TV instead of making sure the whole-grains food program was going right. Then I said that Emmett said that Shapiro better watch his Uranus, not to mention his Venus—or else! Then I walked out even though Smethurst said, "We're not through talking to you, young man!"

I ignored her just like I ignore Mom when she says to men who only want to nail her, "I think I'm in lust with you. Do you lust me?" which she says whenever they eat with me and her at the restaurant when she isn't working. I never say anything but pretend I'm deaf and dumb and eat like a pig and Mom knows now not to get mad and just says, "My son is brain-damaged: just ignore him." But it freaks out a lot of the bastards and I've protected Mom from some real bad cards if you ask me. But Mom doesn't respect me so much and one time she said, "Christopher, when you're a little older I'll listen to you. But right now you're just too young to understand certain adult realities."

"Like what, for instance?" I asked her.

"Loneliness, for one," she said.

"You've got me, don't you?"

"My life doesn't revolve around you."

"Well, I don't care about you either, Mother."

"I didn't say I didn't care."

"You don't love me!"

"I love you more than you'll ever know."

"So how come you took the dirty dancing job last week?"

"It isn't *dirty.* I took it for the money."

"If it isn't dirty, how come you have to take your clothes off?"

"It's artful, Christopher. I'm trying to be artistic and make enough money so we can have our own place. It's hard for women to make money in this sexist society."

I got real mad and screamed, "I think you like being a whore!"

That's when she said "GTF," meaning Going Too Far, so I had to stop or else. I took off on my skateboard with Leon following behind me with a rock in his mouth and went down to Mallory Pier to watch the sun go to New Zealand and listen to Bongo Man with the ring in his nose play drums while his wife danced around with their baby in her arms. Then I watched Lizard Man take his iguanas for a swim on their leashes and then let them crawl around on his bare shoulders.

Everybody who's got a gig at the pier puts a hat on the ground in front of them hoping the tourists will take a picture of them and hit them up with some bread. Me and Buggs once did yo-yo tricks for a week and got a few dollars for it, but some Cuban guy who sold banana bread from his bicycle basket told us we were invading his territory and better watch our *cojones*, so we had to stop yanking our yo-yos in public.

Halloween night I got it on with Termina, Buggs's sister, for the first time. It was cool because she's an older woman. I was dressed like a motorcycle hard ass and wore my dad's captain

hat and a pair of shades and Mom drew skeletons on my arms
with stuff she puts around her eyes to look like a cat and I cut
the sleeves off a shirt so my pits showed like a degenerate. I got
so much candy I could hardly ride Bicycle back at the end of
the night. I let Termina ride with me though because she was
wearing a titty top like an Amazon queen and we went back to
The House where Stanley was throwing a trick-or-treat drug
party in the back on the restaurant patio and he told me and
Buggs and Termina to share the candy because everyone was
pretty wasted and needed some energy, but Termina and Buggs
said, "No way, no day!" so I took my bag and emptied it on
the table and said, "White sugar is dangerous to your health!"
but I was a real hero for letting everyone poison themselves and
they passed me the weed. I took some monster hits and got real
high and made a move on Termina, who was in the kitchen
getting some milk to wash down a peanut butter cup. She let
me rub along her titty top and she opened up when we started
kissing and I could taste the chocolate and peanut butter where
it had got stuck in her molars. It was a pretty heavy scene there
in the kitchen and after she and Buggs left I sat out on the front
porch of The House and freaked out about how much I missed
her after she'd been gone only five minutes when the fact was
I didn't even give a damn about her the day before.

I figured Mom would stay out all night after dancing nudie
and come back in time for breakfast looking like crap with rings
under her eyes and her face muscles soft and puffy, so I stayed
up late. Emmett works from midnight to eight behind the desk,
the "night shaft" as he calls it, and he comes into my room on
nights when Mom's not around and checks on me. He peeks in
and whispers, "It's just me," and I whisper back, "It's just me,
too." And he says, "Go to sleep already, Chris!" and I whisper
back, "I'm trying for Christ's sake!" and keep blowing bubbles
to relax myself. Then he closes the door after saying "God bless
you," and then it's dark again, except for the moonlight coming

through the window or the green light coming from Leon's retarded eyes. It's usually after Emmett closes the door that I cry sometimes without knowing why exactly.

There was a lot of noise from the Halloween party that night, so I couldn't sleep and wound up sitting on the front porch. I passed Murray and Jean who both play on the softball team and wear earrings. They were watching *The Tonight Show* and holding hands. Emmett was on the porch smoking and looking generally flipped out and said that two guests had left because of the noise the "goddamn kids" were making from the restaurant. Emmett was sitting there without a shirt or shoes on, just his huge stomach, and he stared straight ahead and smoked and wheezed. Then he coughed bad and I looked away and afterward I could hear him breathe in and out and it was scary because Emmett looked confused and all white.

I said, "How come Mom dances without no clothes on?"

Emmett looked at me and shrugged. "Christ if I know."

"Is it something she can get in trouble for?"

He lit up another smoke and frowned like he didn't feel too hot. "If they'd only learn to put their goddamn arms around you kids!"

He cut one and apologized, as if Mom being a fucked-up person was his fault. Then he lit a match to get rid of the smell and looked embarrassed.

"What about Mom's dancing?" I said.

"Look, Chris, does the old lady put her goddamn arms around you?"

"Yeah. So what?"

"Then you'll be all right in your life. You won't have worries. When you're older you'll find somebody else to put her arms around you and you'll make it okay."

"How about the other guys she does it to?"

"Does what to?"

"Puts her goddamn arms around!"

"It's good for them, too."

"But she lets them *nail* her!"

Then Emmett said his favorite thing because he didn't know what else to say to me.

"Look, Chris, everyone on this earth is fucked up, so you have to give them each a break."

Stanley didn't give Mom a break though the next morning, even though she is all fucked up. I got up and went to the patio for my buckwheat pancakes. It was raining and the canopy was up and water was dripping off its sides and the place was real crowded because it was Sunday morning. I didn't see Mom working. Kelley was working by herself and seemed really hung over. She wasn't getting it together too cool and was bringing the wrong things to people and spilling coffee. Stanley was in the booth by the orange juice machine and he was reading the paper and looking like he'd pulled an all-nighter the rings were so black under his eyes. He wanted to know where Mom was and I said, "How the hell should I know?"

"She wasn't home last night?"

"Nope. Dancin' for dollars."

He shook his head.

"She's had it, Coke."

I said, *"Adiós, hombre,"* and went out front where Leon was barking and I saw Mom getting out of a car with a man driving. When she came in I pretended I was looking at a plant in the lobby and then I looked up and almost cried I was so mad and she said, "Don't start on me now, son." I just said, "Nice play, Shakespeare!" and she passed me real fast and went straight into the kitchen. I went up to the swinging door and peeked in and could see Mom sitting with Stanley and all he said was, "I know it's a drag, Jody, but I got to X you. This shit is business now." Mom kissed Stanley on the cheek and patted his shoulder because they're friends and then Mom rolled her eyes at Kelley, who winced back because Emmett was substitute waitering and not doing too cool, dropping French toast and a bowl of corn-flakes on the floor, which is a bummer for Stanley because ants always eat and run.

Mom started for the door so I ran out front to the porch. She came out with a cup of coffee and a cigarette and we stared at the rain. Leon stood there with the rock in his mouth and his stupid green eyes and I said to him, "GTF, Leon," but he only wagged his tail and nosed the rock toward me. I said to Mom, "Here's another fine mess." She looked at me vacantly through the cigarette smoke and said, "Gimme a break today, honey." She was freaked. So I tried to be nice instead of honest for once and said, "You'll get your act together and everything will be cool!"

I caught Mom's new act the next week because I heard Kelley and the new waitress, Oakley, talking about going to see Mom dance that night. I waited till I saw them smoking a joint on the sun porch above the restaurant where nobody goes at night and then I got in the back of Kelley's car, which is an old GTO with bucket seats and four on the floor. I laid down low where it was dark and they came along soon, laughing and talking about some guy Oakley knew. She said, "He shot off all over the place just when I thought I'd see the Father, Son, and Holy Ghost, so I gave him the deadly device. He's such a nice boy he was stunned when Sandy joined in. He thinks we're real loosies but I just said, 'This is Key West,'" then Kelley said, "We ought to get it on with Emmett, for mercy's sake. He's so lonely." But Oakley said, "I don't think the bore can get it up anymore!"

They began laughing and I almost got up and brained them both but I figured it was like Dad once said, you gotta love everyone, even flies, so I just hoped Termina didn't turn out like them.

When the car stopped I could hear them both breathing deep and sighing and they were saying, "So fine!" and "Relief is just a rail away!" and "What a vacation head!" Before they got out of the car Kelley said, "I guess we should thank Coke for delivering such fantabulous snow!" and Oakley said, "One and one again, Kells?" and then they were sniffing again and then they were gone and I looked out the window and saw this big red neon sign flashing LIVE NUDE GIRLS, CONTINUOUS SHOW, so I got out and walked between cars and looked around to see if anybody saw me. I was so nervous I took a leak against a car tire and it smelled funny because I'd eaten asparagus for dinner, so I breathed through my mouth and got outta there before somebody smelled me.

I went up to the door of the place which was black and put my ear to it and heard music. Then I heard a hoot and I knew it was Mom and so I opened the door a crack and peeked in. I could see this stage with tables around it and red lights with tons of smoke floating around. Someone behind me said, "Pardon me, Nixon!" and a straight guy in a suit smoking a cigar pushed me away and went inside with a woman. I peeked in again and saw Mom putting money in the jukebox. People were watching her from the tables and pretty soon a record came on and Mom was onstage with beads around her neck and high heels and this black nightgown which you'd expect a movie star to wear. The song was "Stayin' Alive," which I'd heard lots of times at the beach, and then Mom was dancing and pretty soon she loosened her black robe and everyone started hooting and so did Mom and then she flipped her robe up for a second and they all clapped and laughed and hooted. I just opened the door and went in and sat down in the back and nobody even saw me for a while until a waitress started looking at me. I ducked under the table and watched and pretty soon a new song came on and Mom took off her robe so I closed my eyes and couldn't look. Then I felt someone lifting me up and peeked out and it was the bartender. He carried me outside but I didn't open my eyes. I said, "It's cool, man. She's my old lady." But all he said was, "You got a few years before you wanna be hangin' around with broads like these." He let me down real careful and told me to keep it in my pants for a few more years and I just ran across Roosevelt Boulevard, which runs along the beach and that's where I wound up—on the beach, looking at the stars and the water coming in slowly and looking like ink. I just threw rocks into the water for a long time and then I started walking south along the beach back toward The House. I felt real mad at Mom but real sad too. It was fucked up.

I didn't get to The House for a long time because I stopped at Dunkin' Donuts and ate white flour doughnuts and put white sugar in coffee because I had the Sickness unto Death and I played the jukebox because I felt nasty and didn't care if I died from poison food or acted like a moron. I kept wondering how I could get away to New Zealand and get back at Mom. Then I thought about just running away anywhere, but it was so overdone it seemed stupid and I didn't feel like getting mugged or suckered out of stuff by strangers who don't know you and are even worse to you sometimes than people who supposedly love you.

I stayed in Dunkin' Donuts pigging out and then a waitress woke me up and it was light out so I hitched a ride by some lady on a Harley-Davidson 1000 and the lady told me to hang on to her tight. She put my hands on her tits and so I kept them there but didn't squeeze because I figured she might get hot and start moaning and crack up the cycle and break both our asses in three quarters. I just put my face into her back and held on to her two big ones and when I finally got off she said I was real cute and I said thanks and then she was gone and I was only two blocks from The House. I understood now what Emmett meant about people just putting their goddamn arms around one another, and then I got the hots for Termina.

•   •   •

Mom was in the lobby talking with Emmett when I showed up. I heard Emmett tell Mom not to knock on the doors of the other guests and wake them up and Mom said the guy was a writer and wrote late at night anyway and that she was only looking for me. Emmett asked Mom if she thought he was a fool or something because Emmett said Mom was spaced out more than an astronaut when she came home last night and that she better not come into the lobby anymore in that black dancing gown because she'd only get herself or one of the guests in trouble. Mom said okay okay already that she was sorry and then Emmett said he didn't blame me for running away. Then I came pushing through the screen doors keeping my eyes real low and just mumbled howdy and went past them toward the kitchen and Mom said, "Christopher Crosse!"—which is my real name—"you come talk to your mother!" I turned around like I was skidding on my bike and made a noise with my mouth and gave her my bad eyes. She blushed and said, "Don't you look at me like that," and I said, "I want my picture back," which meant the picture of me standing by Blair's garage next to Leon that I gave her for a birthday present and Mom said, "Why?" and all I said was "Whore!" and Mom said, "Don't you walk away from me!" I turned and said, "Ah, for God's sake, Mother!" and Emmett winked at me, meaning I should be cool because people don't live forever, so I just shook my head from side to side and went into the kitchen where I found Stanley and Sandy, the maid who made the beds, working the tables alone. Stanley was mad as hell and Jetty told me that Stanley was PO'd because Oakley and Kelley had smashed up his car and had been arrested for drunken driving. Lewis was smoking a J and said, "DWI is the pits. They come down hard on you." I said, "They come down hardon Mom, too," and Lewis said, "Pipe down, clown!" and hit me with a raw egg on the shoulder. Jetty told Lewis to act his age not his IQ, and then

Jetty told me to mop up the floor and I said I'd take him to court for child abuse. Then Stanley came in and shouted, "Cut the shit and get table three's fondue!" Lewis said, "Oh fuck!" and picked up a pan where the fondue was burning and Jetty looked at Lewis and Lewis looked at both of them and gave the gladiator sign with a thumb down, meaning the shit had hit the fan. Jetty went to the patio and lied that the stove had screwed up and that they would have to evacuate the kitchen because of a gas leak until tomorrow. Everybody left and Stanley and Lewis and Jetty and me went up to the sun porch and blew a few Js and then they decided to hit the beach and do frisbee and snorkeling and just try to mellow out and take a pass on the day. I put the OUT TO LUNCH sign up on the kitchen door and shut off the lights and a couple of people came in expecting to eat and when they saw the sign one guy said, "This brand of irony is positively tiresome!" and the other guy said, "Oh hush. We'll just go cruising for that bangle bracelet you've always adored."

I went to Mom's room and mine and took my picture from her wallet. In the picture I was standing up in dungaree shorts and basketball socks to my knees in my red Converse high tops and I didn't have a shirt on, only my long hair to my shoulders that was real light from the sun. I looked like a pretty weirded-out person for seven, skinny and not too happy, but I figured it was a sexy picture since I didn't have a shirt on, so I decided to give it to Termina. I wrote "Born to Run!" on the back and went to school late to see her and give her the picture and The Worst didn't even send me to Sadist's when I walked in at eleven. Everyone was flipped out about my power, especially me, because I was chewing gum, too, but all Smethurst said was "Fold your papers in half and number one to twenty in the left-hand margin." She sounded like a computer and I didn't get one answer right. One question was "Who is the richest man in

America?" and I wrote "Some Capitalist Pig who rips off people like us!"

I saw Termina at lunch and Buggs was telling her how The Worst didn't even say anything to me when I came in late only got real red and Termina laughed and looked at me and made me get red, but I also felt cool. Then I said I wanted to tell Termina something alone, so Buggs pretended to be a mental midget and galloped away slapping his ass. I told Termina I knew she was older and all that and I was her brother's friend and all that but I wanted her to have this—so I gave her the picture and she said I was a real doll and we should "get it on sometime." I said, "I'm hip to that trip," and she said maybe next weekend and I said my Mom worked weekend nights, so we could always go to my place. She said, "We'll see about that, young man!" since I was one year younger than her in school.

I was real happy but a little freaked out about getting it on with Termina because I never really had before except once with a girl who was just a friend. We did a little strip show for each other and then we kissed, but it didn't seem too great except it was weird seeing a person without a wang even though wangs are pretty gross little pissers themselves, but I was only eight then and two years makes a big difference even if nothing changes except your attitude.

I took Leon with me on Zodiac and went racing all around Curry's Dock out to where the cargo boat sank off the reef a couple of years ago. I was moving pretty fast and Leon gave me that look of his, so I slowed up and looked down at the reef at the turtle grass and the sponges and once three barracuda shot by like torpedoes. I cut the engine and lay back and talked to Leon and caught some rays and pretended we were on a raft to New Zealand. Then I pressed my fingers against my eyelids and saw stars instead of orange light and it was like I was floating toward the sun. Then I smoked a J and blew it up Leon's nose so he could get off too, and after that we were both totally mellow and laid back and happy. By the time I got to *Tchandee* to pick up the snapper I was cocky and told Snyder I wasn't getting paid enough. He said maybe a knuckle sandwich would do the trick and I said I was only jokin' 'cause I'd been tokin' but he didn't seem too happy about it. When he climbed down with the fish I saw this naked lady lean over the side and when she saw me staring she said, "What's happenin', cutie?" I realized she was the lady who gave me the feel on the cycle. I asked Snyder who she was and he put his hand to my face and said, "Smell that?" and I said, "Yeah?" and he said, "That's my old lady!" Then he grabbed my arm and got me in a chicken wing and told me to tell his wife to "practice hygiene!" so I said real low, "Practice hygiene," and he said, "Tell her to scrub up for her man!" and bent my arm some more so I had to yell, "Scrub up! Scrub up!" Then he let me go and when I looked up I saw his wife gobbing down at us and I just took the fish and started the engine. Snyder said, "Thanks, me boy; did I hurt you any?" I said no but felt like crying because the bastard had scared the hell out of me.

When Leon and me got back to Curry's Dock I saw that Leon had started eating one of the fish, so I pushed him away saying, "Cut the crap, kid!" but the fish was ruined and bloody at the head, so after I docked Zodiac I sat on the wharf and checked out the fish. They were okay except the one with the bad head. I took it off the gill lock and started to chuck him back in the water when I noticed some thread sticking out of him. Then I could see his whole belly was tied up and so I sat down under a palm and saw that all the snappers were sewed up in the stomach though it wasn't real obvious or anything. I opened up the bloody fish all the way and found this white powder wrapped in a sandwich baggy. I couldn't figure it out other than to know something fishy was going on behind locked gills! I scratched my head and tried to figure out what was what. I opened the bag and put it to my nose and sniffed it and some went up my nostrils and burned a little. I tried a little taste of it and pretty soon my tongue didn't feel like it was there anymore, or like I'd been to the dentist to have a tooth pulled and he'd given me the needle. My nose felt like it does when it's cold outside and I kept sniffing like I was sick and it reminded me of nights on the patio of The House during softball parties when everyone walked around like they had enough snot to start a plague. So I figured I'd found out something I wasn't supposed to have and that was how come Snyder told me not to be cute. I didn't know what to do about the missing fish and the bag I had in my hand, though I figured I'd better tell Jetty about it, but then I got an amazing idea that made my heart beat fast, so I just put the fish in the basket of Bicycle and rode home standing up as you have to do on Key West bikes if you're a kid because of the butterfly handlebars.

When I got back to The House I brought Jetty the fish and he gave me two Js and a five to buy an album. He said, "Thanks. Now beat it," so I did, hoping he wouldn't count the fish. The next day I was real scared to go into breakfast but when he saw me he called me "little troll of misery" and didn't say anything bad so I figured it was cool. I had hid the stuff in a finger of my ball glove and put it in the very back of the closet with some of Mom's crap. Since it was Saturday after breakfast I went to Emmett's house with my glove on like I was off to play ball and Emmett was in the kitchen eating enough for a large family. He was smoking as usual and looked pretty lonesome and he was cursing and trying to figure out what he called "accounts payable." He said something about "damn kids so high they can't count to ten," and when I sat down he gave me some rose hip tea and lemon and honey and I just watched him adding for a while and eating four bananas and a whole loaf of toasted carrot cake. Then he looked up and said, "What's cookin', kid?" in his shaky voice with sad eyes like a basset hound, and I didn't know whether or not I should tell him. I said, "If I show you something you swear to God you won't tell anyone?" He said, "Jesus Christ, Chris, don't tell me then!" I felt a little weirded out but said, "I got to show it to you. It's nothing real heavy." He said, "Okay, I swear to God," and lit another cigarette and folded his hands on his stomach and leaned back and stared at me, so I took out the bag from my glove and said, "What is this?" and he took the bag and put it to his nose to smell it. Then he put some on his gums and looked at me suspiciously.

"Leon found it!" I said.

"Where?"

"Came home with it in his mouth."

"You telling the truth?"

"What is it already!" I just looked at the bag in his hand and then looked up fast at him.

"Toot," he said.

"Huh?"

"Coke." He looked down at it again.

"Give it back now." I put out my hand and he gave it to me.

"You have plans for this?"

"Ask me no questions, I'll tell you no lies."

"You want to go to jail?"

"Maybe!"

"Who you mad at, Chris—me?"

"I wanna help Mom" was all I said. "I wanna get some bread so she can stop dancing."

He nodded to the bag. "You've got a gram in that bag."

"Is that good?"

"Costs about ninety in Miami."

"Cents?"

"Bucks, kid."

I looked down at the bag in my hand and then I stuffed it back in my glove.

"I'll give you a hundred for it right now," Emmett said.

"You can have it for fifty."

Emmett looked right at me. "Jo come home with it, Chris?"

"Leon found it! Leon!"

"Okay," he said softly. "I'll take it for fifty. I don't want you in trouble." He took out two twenties and a ten from his wallet and looked at me. I stashed the money and took off. Before I reached outside I heard Emmett flush the toilet.

There was a day game at the park so I had to run the stand and I tried to sell organic raisins and figs that Emmett brought down, but people wanted brownies and pretzels with BHT and lard in them, so I gave up trying to sell the fruit and gave them away to the kids again in hopes of turning them on to trying stuff. Then Emmett brought down some humus, which you make from chickpeas and tahini butter and lots of garlic, and some people bought that on whole-wheat bread with sprouts instead of hot dogs with sheep eyes in them. Emmett tried to talk to people about how hypoglycemia was making them alcoholics and neurotics and how it was ruining society, but one woman said the problem was bad interpersonal vibes not bad food that was messing up people. Emmett said the two were the same, but most people just frowned at him and said to me, "Gimme a footer with the hot stuff, Coke."

The House played in the second game and Oakley and Kelley who just got out of jail because Stanley bailed them out with big bucks were in the stands and so was Stephanie and Mom. They were all talking about how Oakley and Kelley had smashed in the GTO and how weird it was being in jail in a cage. Then Oakley screamed, "Come on, Jetty, come on, Jetty! You can strike 'em out. You can get 'em!" because Jetty was pitching for The House. Reggie the umpire who's got no teeth screamed, "Stah-wike fwee!" and jumped around with his hand in the air. His cap fell off and everyone in the stands cracked up like epileptic cases and chucked empty beer cans at the screen behind home plate and screamed, "Weggie! Weggie! Weggie!" So Reggie finally grabbed his underpants strap and winked at them. It was very pathetic.

Termina came by to say she still wanted to get it on, so I said "Far out!" and closed up an inning early, since The House was sixteen runs ahead and most everyone had split. I went up to Mom in the stands and said I wanted to talk with her. She was with Pat and he was drunk as hell and said to me, "How's it hangin', pal?" and I said, "Like Tarzan's rope, dope!" He nodded and said to Mom, "I dig your kid, baby!" and I felt like saying, "I'd like to dig your grave!" but I knew Mom would say "GTF" so I just zipped it up and helped Mom down the bleachers because she was loaded and had trouble walking and probably had taken some 'ludes, which really messed her up and made her eyes look Chinese. "I got some work money for you," I said, "so pretty soon you can quit dancin', okay?" and I gave her thirty bucks of the fifty. She said, "Where'd you get this money?" and I said, "Earned it, damnit!" She smiled and said, "Keep it, it's yours." I said, "Don't sweat it, Mom. There's more comin'." She shook her head like she was impressed and I said, "Pretty soon you can quit being a live nude girl!" Then she got mad and said, "I like dancing, Christopher." I said, "It's not your trip to strip!" and she said "GTF" and slapped me on the ass like she loved me and squinted her eyes like she does when she's thinking about crying, so I just stopped and remembered people don't live forever. Then Termina came out of the LADIES, so I asked Mom when she'd be home and she said, "Don't know," and told me to eat dinner at the restaurant with Stanley and Kelley. I said, "Maybe, maybe not," and left with Termina.

We went to a seafood place where you could get stuff at a booth without a waitress coming over and making you feel embarrassed. It was an outdoor place, too, which was good because it was romantic and you could smell the gas from the tour boats that was all over the water. I ate salad and grilled cheese and Termina ate a lobster, which pretty much made me want to cry because you could see the lobster's eyes and tentacles and I kept thinking that a lobster had a heart too and that it was pretty horrible to make a lobster's heart stop beating and living just so you could dip his muscles in butter sauce, and hearing Termina open its body by breaking its shell and ripping off its legs and claws grossed me out and made me think Dad was wrong to believe in God if He let lobsters die in boiling water when they were still alive. But Termina was nice and said she hoped I didn't mind that she was eating a lobster and I lied and said I respected that she was into a different trip than me, which was actually a crock, but sex makes you a bullshit artist.

After dinner when it was dark we went to South Beach and Termina said a friend of hers had an orgasm and I said, "That's too bad," because I didn't know what it meant and thought that her friend maybe had a tumor or something. She said it happens when you make love and I said I was only joking. We got stoned on the Js Jetty gave me and tried to forget about how weird life was. I showed her some baseball cards I always kept in my pocket and we were so stoned we really got into studying the backgrounds in the pictures! Later on we tongue-kissed and I felt around and she had hair on her beaver, making it a bush, which made me feel pretty bad since I didn't have any on my snake. But I made her think it was cool when she got down there because I told her I got crabs at The House like everyone else from the whore from Miami and had to get shaved, so I got out of it pretty smooth because she bought it totally and I didn't have to tell her that I didn't know what else to do with your hose other than water a tree trunk when nobody was looking.

Sunday a band plays at Sand's Beach and everyone from The House goes there when the kitchen closes at two. It's like a big family day and I dig it and so does Mom, who dances in the sand when the band plays. I mostly play frisbee with Buggs and Leon and Mom lets me take a few hits from her Bloody Mary but says if I'm going to get high I should go somewhere where people aren't hip to it. Some older people are down on kids tokin', but Mom isn't because she says all people should be free to get Key Wasted.

But I didn't get stoned that day. For a long time me and Buggs sat at the end of the dock watching show-offs surfsailing. Boats kept landing on the dock and some of the women who got off were real heart-stoppers. Buggs liked to whistle at them and then point to me and say, "He did it! He did it!" Buggs has a hard time relating to women as human beings.

Some lady got off a Pacemaker motor yacht with twin 671 diesels and me and Buggs croaked ten times apiece because she didn't have a top on and she winked at me and I winked back. When she got to the beach though she put on this T-shirt so it wasn't illegal or any of that crap, which Mom says is strictly uptight white rules and anything related to the body and sex when people are consenting should never be illegal, though Mom says sado stuff like when people use whips and chains and brass knuckles and stuff like that is pretty sick and she could personally never get into it. Personally I think taking your clothes off in front of a bunch of strangers and dancing to a jukebox is pretty sick myself, but Termina says it's Mom's karma to be a LIVE NUDE GIRL. Termina's mom, Sorolta, is an astrologer, and Termina says Mom's weird life isn't something I should let mess up my head since it's inevitable. But the problem isn't with my head but my heart. I never could talk my heart into something it didn't want to feel.

Anyway, I was on the dock with Buggs checking out a man-o'-war blob on the water when Jetty came out to meet some dude who had pulled up in the Pacemaker motor yacht with the topless lady. Jetty went aboard walking real slow, so I knew he

was stoned out and also because when he passed me he said,
"Never fear, boys, you're living in Eternal Mind!" Whenever he
says flipped-out stuff like that I know he's stoned bad, so I said,
"Earth to Jetty, Earth to Jetty!" and he mumbled, "Dig it,
baby!" and dragged on a cigarette like it was great to inhale
poison. He spoke to some guy who was real skinny and wore
a Tarzan bathing suit so his snake could be seen by all the
chicks, though I figured he was probably Ray the Gay except
I saw with my own eyes his girl friend come to shore, so I
guessed maybe he was half-and-half. Mom says a lot of people
are into that since it improves your chances of scoring, but I
think it's pretty gross except maybe it's not so bad since less
guys will want to nail Mom when she's high.

I watched Jetty shake hands with this guy who was wearing
sunglasses because it was really sunny and hot and it was weird
how this guy reached for Jetty's hand with his left hand that
was full of rings. He sounded like what Emmett says is a Fire
Island dialect with a little Frisco thrown in. They were sitting
in chairs smoking cigarettes.

"Let me be discreet," the guy said. "Has Jetty done his
thing?"

Jetty nodded.

"Oh fine. Jetty's been a good boy. All right then, let me ask
what quantity Jetty is anticipating?"

"Depends," Jetty said.

"Listen, doll, this isn't salesman time. This stuff is *monster*!"

Jetty looked at the ocean. "I don't know if it's monster," he
said. "You can do a one-and-one if you want."

"I've been running for seventy-two hours," the guy said.
"Can't you hear it in my voice? Doesn't that tell you the entire
story!"

"What?"

"This stuff is *God,* Jetty!"

"Listen," Jetty said, "one g for nine zero."

"One g?"

"You got it, Ira."

"Nine zero is a rather strange figure. Is the nose really worth Miami prices?"

"Tourist season, Ira."

"Who's copping here, doll? I presumed I was carrying the bags."

Jetty said, "Come on, man. Fleece just told me you were nomad."

"I was under the conception you were talking Hi Ho Silver."

"We don't play with that stuff, Ira." Jetty stood up and told Ira "Later, fella" and got back on the pier and passed us with a wink and rolled his eyes. Me and Buggs didn't hang around the pier because Ira was looking at us so we split like schizos and played Army Deserters in Sweden on the beach by getting high and pretending we couldn't go back to America and were really bummed out by society. We looked around for blondes like you'd find in Sweden but we didn't see any so the game got boring and we bagged it. We flipped frisbee and then rode our bikes to White Street Fishing Pier and played Demolition Maniacs by riding really fast down the street and over the pier into the water. We had to quit pretty soon though when Buggs cracked his lip on the handlebar of the bike on his second crash because he tried to dodge Leon who was jumping in with him. So we went home and ate yogurt and blew another J and watched color TV in the lobby of The House with Murray and Jean, the two guys on the softball team who live together and wear earrings.

Monday Termina came by The House so we could walk to school after lunch. It was strange not going back with Buggs but with his sister instead, and all alone with her, too, so I figured she had something to tell me without wanting Buggs around, and sure enough she said that our get-it-on signal should be twiddling thumbs so that if we were ever in a crowd and wanted to make it together we would know how to tell the other person without anyone else knowing or something very embarrassing like that, and I said, "Sock it to me, baby!"

Before we got to school the sun came out and without clouds around it anymore, and the thought of listening to The Worst made me think of being trapped in a hot room with no air with a crippled person taking a crap, so I told Termina I was taking Zodiac out instead, and she said what about her, so I said I don't care if you want to come, then come, so she came with me to Curry's Dock. We went out just toolin' around until we stopped at Pine Island across from Mallory Pier, where all the freaks always groove out on the sunset. Termina started twiddlin' her thumbs when we got on the rocks of the island and I smiled back and a little later she said did I know what a blow job was, and I said that's how you make glasses and Termina smiled and said, "You mean how you make somebody's cup runneth over!" I said, "What?" and she said didn't I ever hear about Phil Latio and Connie Lingus? I said, "Huh?" and after she said it straightforward I almost fainted and asked her how come people did this and she said, "So you can make each other have orgasms and feel great and happy."

I was pretty freaked out, so I said I think we should go because I had to get fish at *Tchandee,* and Termina said she had never gone fishing but had been a master baiter for two years now. She took my hand and said, "Oh Phil, just relax and let me show you." And after that I called Termina Connie and I was known as Phillip, as in fill her up.

We got the fish from Snyder and I introduced him to Termina by saying, "This is Connie," and he said, "Connie who?" and I said, "Connie Lingus!" He looked at me narrowing his eyes and said, "Wise guys die young." Then he said, "Be careful, Coke!" and climbed up the gunwale. I looked up for his wife's jugs but she wasn't around, so Termina and me went back to the pier. Then we walked to the Turtle Kraals because Termina had never seen George the biggest loggerhead turtle in captivity. We watched George for a while and then I saw that Termina had a snapper in her hand she had taken off the gill lock and she threw it in before I could say anything to her. I watched George eat the fish and figured he'd be feeling no pain for a while even if he did weigh eight hundred pounds. Somebody yelled at Termina for feeding the turtles and she said, "Don't let him talk that way to me, Phil!" so I told the guy that Termina was my retarded sister and didn't know how to read the DO NOT FEED THE TURTLES sign. He told me to watch her better then or leave, so we did, and I figured it had cost me ninety dollars to show Termina George.

Except then I figured it was Jetty's powder not mine and I figured I'd just take another fish and not sweat the small stuff. Then me and Termina tongue-kissed behind the package store before I delivered the goods to Jetty minus two fish. I played Rock with Leon and blew half a bottle of bubbles because without Termina's hands on my ass I felt scared shitless about stealing from Jetty and couldn't keep cool about it.

Before I left for the stand that night Jetty told me to come into the kitchen after dinner and I freaked out and had to smoke a cigarette in the bathroom where everyone got crabs. But Jetty just gave me this bag and told me to take it to the stand and that the catcher of Max's Muffler team would come by for it. I asked him what it was and he said, "Brewer's yeast," and opened the brown bag and said, "See." I saw it was white powder so I said, "Far out," feeling scared that he was going to say something to me, but it was okay and when I got to the stand later I put my finger in the powder and tasted it and sure enough my tongue got numb, so I knew it wasn't Brewer's yeast but coke. I figured Jetty really didn't care about me because if

I ever got caught I was really screwed, so I didn't feel bad about ripping him off. I hid the bag behind the Coke machine and when the catcher came by and said he wanted the Brewer's yeast I said, "Okay, I got it right next to the Coke!" and he got red for a second, but I didn't say any more and he seemed to think I was just stupid, not a smart ass.

I tried to sell all vegetable-protein hot dogs called Vegalinks that night instead of the real sheep-eye ones, but people thought I was nuts and someone tore down the sign I'd made with Termina which said EAT YOUR LOVER NOT A DEAD ANIMAL. This kid with acne called me a stupid asshole and I said, "Get off my case or I'll punch your face," even though he was older and bigger and he said, "Okay, jerk-off, hit me, man!" He started coming around to the door where only employees could come in so I screamed. Stanley was watching the game and he gimped over on his bad leg from 'Nam and got to me just as the zit bastard caught me in a headlock and was about to give me a nuggie treatment. Stanley got him in a karate pressure point behind the ear and the kid started to cry and curse Stanley, but Stanley let him go and said he was an undercover cop and if this kid ever touched me again he'd arrest him for assault and being ugly in public and lock him up, and when the kid got three steps away from Stanley he screamed, "Up your ass with Mobile gas!" and just walked away like he was cool and not scared. But he was crying and his face was white from being frightened so his zits looked purple instead of red.

Next day I went to South Beach with one thing in mind and when I saw some fellow longhairs who I knew weren't locals I sat on a towel near them and listened. One of them said, "I'm really into gettin' Key Wasted this week, man!" and the other said, "I know how you feel, bro'!" so I took a deep breath and went up to them and said, "Howdy!" and they said, "What's happenin', man!" like I was a little fool who they could goof on.

But I sat down with them and said, "You dudes wanna do a J?" and they said, "Posolutely, *hombre!*" so we did a J though I didn't take much in because I didn't want to be too high and tried to be cool the way Jetty was on the boat with the Fire Island dude. I said, "You guys hip to a little one-and-one?" One of the guys whose hair was a black Afro said, "You got girls or something?" and I said, "A little nose action does help with chicks, right?" And I started sniffing like I had a cold so his friend, who had long red hair and a mustache said, "You serious, man? Toot?" and I said, "Man-o'-wars get it on in water?" and he said, "How much, kid?"

"For a g," I whispered, "nine zero."

"Don't be so tough," the guy with the Afro said, but his friend was hip to things and said, "We'll give you seventy-five a gram, man, no more."

"Eighty or nothing," I said, and the red-haired guy said, "Where do we toot?" I didn't know what else to say so I said, "This stuff is really monster!" and then I got scared and my leg was shaking but the red-haired guy said his car was good, so when we got inside I took out the bag and he had a penknife with him and dipped it in and put some on a book and made two lines of it. Then he found a straw on the floor and sucked the stuff up his nose and put his head back and in about five minutes he was sniffing and said, "A mighty fine set of rails!" Then he wanted to know who I worked for and all I said was "Please, just gimme the money now, okay." I gave him the bag and he got his wallet out of the glove compartment and said, "All I got is two fifties," and I said, "I'll get change." He said, "Where?" and I pointed to the restaurant by the beach. "I trust you," he said, and I said, "We're all in this fucked-up world together!" I went into the restaurant and got five tens for one of the fifties, saying my dad was on the beach and needed change, so I got the eighty bucks I asked for and the two dudes got their coke. We shook hands soul style on the beach and the guy with the Afro said, "Maybe we'll see you around again, huh?" and I said, "Never can tell," and the hip guy with the red hair said, "Let's do business," and then I took off on Bicycle feeling proud and happy about being able to make it in the real world.

At dinner Jetty finally served snapper to the carnivores and he didn't say anything to me and neither did Snyder who came to dinner too. A lot of people had runny noses at dinner, including Mom and Oakley and Kelley and Lewis. Emmett told me they had runny noses because they were sick in the head and I winked at Emmett because I was hip now.

After Mom finished working dinner I was in the room with her while she was getting dressed for dancing and I asked her how much she made a week stripping. She said it depended on tips and I said how much with the best tips and she said if she worked regular three nights a week she made seventy-five dollars plus tips, which sometimes made it over one hundred bucks or a little more, so I said, "If I make that much on my own will you quit dancing?"

"How you gonna do that?"

"You can't ask any questions," I said.

"You gettin' in trouble?" she said.

"Just answer me what I asked."

"I like dancing, Christopher. Why should I stop?"

I looked out the window and kept my eyes there because Mom was putting on makeup and I didn't like it on her, 'specially the crud around her eyes that made her look like a cat.

"You won't stop then?"

"You've got to let me live my life," she said. "I let you live yours, don't I?"

I tried to get out of the room real fast but Mom grabbed me by the arm and said, "What?" and I said, "Lemme go," but it was too late because I was crying and couldn't stop.

"Christopher Crosse," she said, "how come you're always

guilt trippin' me?" But I couldn't talk because I was crying, so I just buried my head in Mom's shoulder and held on tight and tried to forget where we were and how Mom and me lived and why Dad was gone. Then I got tough with myself and stood up and moved away and said, "Never mind about me. It's a sex problem. I don't want to talk about it."

"She isn't pregnant, is she?" Mom joked. I wiped my eyes and said, "I gotta marry her and that's that." Then I raced from the room through the lobby past Emmett who was watering plants and Stanley who was bawling out Sandy the maid for not cleaning the toilets with enough Mr. Clean. Leon followed me off the porch and we ran to the city cemetery and I cried some more because I was really mad and didn't know what to do. I wished I'd have a close encounter of the third kind so that a spaceman would take me away from my life, but the only thing that landed near me was a horse fly.

Next day I went to school all day and got back two Fs on a geography quiz and a vocabulary test, and after school Jetty was on the front porch smoking a cigarette taking a break from work and said, "No more fish for a while," and I said, "Why not!" and he said, "Yellow snapper ain't selling worth shit in the restaurant." I said, "Why not try some other kind?" and he said, "Couple of days maybe." Then he said, "Look, Coke, I got some manicotti noodles some people in town want so you wanna deliver 'em for me for a couple of Js?" I said, "Sure," so we went into the kitchen and he gave me these three white boxes in bags and said, "They'll each give you an envelope with bread in them. Just bring them back to me, okay?" Then Jetty gave me fifty cents and said, "Buy a Guru Chew, you dig 'em, right?" and I said, *"Gracias,"* and rode off with the addresses in my head because Jetty said I'd just better remember them that's all. I checked one of the boxes out behind a tree at the end of the block and saw inside that it was coke not manicotti noodles, but I delivered them anyway and didn't take any because I figured people would complain and I'd get caught. I delivered them to people I'd seen eating at the restaurant and they gave me an envelope just like Jetty said without me even asking. I bought a Guru Chew and came back to The House and Jetty and me blew a joint on the sun deck before dinner began. Mom was there talking to this new guest who was the writer she liked and she laughed at everything he said and hardly noticed me or Jetty.

Mom and the writer were at the softball game that night sitting in the stands drinking poison beer and laughing. I sold ten humus sandwiches and six tabuli sandwiches that Emmett had made. He came down late to see how his stuff was selling and we both agreed the humus and tabuli could catch on, and he talked about how legumes were good for you and grains too in combination and kept talking about how meat was bad because it had DES in it and nitrites and that meat also made ammonia in your intestines and gave you cancer. I told him GTF because he was starting to scare me because Mom and Termina ate meat sometimes. Then he said the thing to do was get the kids off the crap and that he was trying to get some of the schools to start vegetarian meal programs, so I said if he was so into health how come he smoked? He said, "Sometimes if you can't help yourself it makes you try extra hard to help other people." I kept watching Mom and the writer from The House who Emmett said was a novelist and I said, "What's that?" and Emmett said, "A person who writes stories," and I said, "Big goddamn deal!" because I didn't like the way he was sitting so close to Mom.

Before I closed up Mom and the writer came by and I asked Mom if she'd like to go to a horror movie at the mall, which is a gross-out kingdom but has good flicks, and she said maybe tomorrow that she was going dancing tonight at the Bull with the writer. I said, "What time you comin' home?" and she said,

"Don't know," and I said, "Make it midnight, okay?" and she said, "Probably much later," and I said, "It's only nine. How much can you dance, for Christ's sake!" She said, "GTF," and I said, "Go on then already or you'll be out all night again!"

Emmett and me watched TV till late and right before I went to bed the writer came in without Mom so I said, "Where's Missus Crosse?" and he said, "Still dancin', g' night." He was loaded. I hugged Emmett good night and he patted the back of my head and whispered, "That's it, kid, just put your arms around someone." He smelled of tobacco and was warm and fat, and when I went to my room I saw the writer leave the bathroom and go into his room just down the hall. I went to take a leak myself and when I got in there I noticed how he had peed all over the floor he was so drunk.

I fell asleep and then I was waked up by knocking, so I opened the door and I saw Mom knocking on the writer's door. She was whispering, "Lemme in, damnit!" and after a couple more minutes she knocked again and said, "I won't stay long, damnit!" but the door didn't open at all and finally she came back to the room. When she saw me standing there she said, "Why hello, sweetie pie!" She stank like a beer keg so I just turned away and got into my sleeping bag and didn't say a word. Mom had a cigarette before she went to bed and I said, "At least brush your teeth for God's sake!" but Mom just put the light out and pretty soon she was snoring like Emmett breathes when he's awake because he's got emphysema.

In the morning Stanley told Mom it wasn't too cool to knock on a guest's door and Mom said, "Look, I wasn't knockin' on anyone's door last night!" and I think she believed herself. Stanley just shook his head and said, "You're never gonna get it together, Jody!" All I said was "Ditto."

I figured it'd be pretty wacked out on my part to tool over all my bread to Mom since all she was going to do with it was drink and keep dancing it away, so I went to the bank during lunch hour and opened a savings account. The lady, Miss Brama-zerro, was a real straight person and started asking twenty million questions for the FBI or something, which surprised me because I figured she'd be more than happy to get my bread. She asked me my name and I said Chris Crosse and she said was that my real name, so I said my real name was Christopher Crosse but that she could call me Jesus H. Christ if she got her kicks that way. Then she asked me about my parents and what they did and when I told her Dad was in a monastery in New Zealand she didn't believe me, so I said, "Look, I'm not shitting you, okay?" She asked me about Mom and I said, "Dancer," and then she asked me about me and I said I was the success story in the family and that I operated a health-food stand at the ball park and that's when I dumped the hundred bucks on the desk between us figuring that now she'd treat me with a little respect. But all she did was say, "I can't take your money, Mr. Crosse, until you have it co-signed by a parent or guard-ian." So I said, "Listen, I'm a busy man. I'm on lunch break," and she said, "Don't you go to school?" and I said, "Gimme a break, lady; I *gotta* go to school—where you think I'm on break from!" So she said, "Sorry, Mr. Crosse, but rules are rules." I told her rules were made to be busted but all she said was, "Not here at City Savings!" I just shook my head and left because I could see she was a total robot who probably thought drinking cocktails on a patio was hot shit.

But I know when they've got me by the short hairs even though I don't have any, so I rode Bicycle to The House and had Emmett sign the form and then I went back to the bank and Miss Bramazerro gave me a bank book that said I had a hundred big ones in the vault. She also said something about interest, but I was too cool for my own good and said, "I ain't interested!" and split with my book and hid it back in my room. Then I went to school and The Worst was talking about the

"Middle-Western states in America" so I started playing this football game I made up, which is too hard to explain but all you need is to make lots of circles and then try to make straight lines between the circles without changing the direction of the lines more than eight times before you make the end zone at the end of the paper. But The Worst asked me to stand up and tell the class something about what she was talking about and Buggs whispered she was talking about corn, so I stood up and said, "They grow lots of corn in the Middle West of America."

Smethurst got cute and said, "Who's they?"

"They the farmers," I said.

"What else?" She seemed pretty mad I'd gotten out of the jam.

"They feed corn to many farm animals like pigs and cows that they the farmers slaughter by cutting off their heads and breaking their legs and bodies and people who eat these dead bodies of these murdered animals who are fed corn are called carnivores and they are the true gross-out pigs of America. The End!"

*"Go to the principal's office!"*

Buggs was really cracking up and so were some other people and so she said, "And you too, Mr. Sivil!" and he said "Thanks!" so we both left arm in arm going down between the aisles. We didn't go to Sadist's office but just went straight to the beach and played frisbee with Leon running between us trying to catch it.

I saw the two who'd bought the cocaine from me and I gave them the peace sign and the hip guy came up to me and said, "What's your name anyway?" but I didn't want to tell them because maybe they'd tell Mom so I just said, "Call me Coke." He said, "What can you do for our friends, Coke?" and he pointed to two other guys and these two guys came up to us. One had curly brown hair with lots of freckles on his face and seemed old as Stanley, and another guy had blond hair like a California surfer and he also looked pretty old, so I got nervous, but they seemed hip and gave me a soul shake, which Jetty taught me to do after you've smoked weed with a stranger and want to split but want to seem friendly, or if you just meet somebody and want to cop weed then a soul shake means you're hip to what's happening. The blond guy said, "You shuffle soapers or reds?"

"What?"

"You know, man," the brown-haired guy said.

"Just nose," I said, real scared.

"Any horse ridin' through town?" the blond guy asked.

"Horse?"

"You know, man!" The brown-haired guy winked.

I started away. "I can't talk now, okay?"

The red-haired guy who bought stuff from me said, "They're basically just interested in toot."

"Maybe," I said.

"Ten g's worth," the brown-haired guy said.

I stopped. "Ten g's!"

"Ten too many for you to handle?" the blond guy asked.

"Maybe."

"We'll give you seven a g," the brown-haired guy said.

"You mean seventy bucks a bag!"

"Hey man!" The blond guy looked around and winced. "I thought you wanted to be cool. You fucking with our craniums?"

"Sorry," I said.

"Look," the brown-haired guy said, "we'll give you five hundred for ten grams."

"You said seventy a bag!" My heart really was going berserk and I told myself not to let these dudes hustle me so I said, "It's eight a bag or nothing."

"Ten g's is a pretty heavy catch," the blond guy said.

"You heard me," I said. Buggs started coming over to see what was up.

"You take a check?" the blond guy said.

"A candle burn up a turtle's nose!" I said, real pissed-off sounding.

"Hey, listen man," the blond guy said. "We're not interested in shafting anybody."

I said, "Green stuff, mister!"

I flipped the frisbee to Buggs to keep him away and waved that he should move back. I walked away from the three. My heart was making it hard for me to breathe. The blond guy said, "My name's Krystle. How's this Thursday right here sound?"

I said, "Thursday's Thanksgiving."

He said, "I know, man, but room rates double Thursday and we're splittin'. Whataya say?"

I thought and said, "Okay."

"Here?"

"Queer Pier," I said. "Two o'clock sharp."

I spun the frisbee into the ocean and raced in after it. It was good to be underwater where it was real quiet and the sand was all white and rippled from waves, and all I could think of was getting that eight hundred bucks and giving some to Mom and taking the other half and going to New Zealand to find Dad. Then I was so scared I almost cried and choked on salt water and had to surface for air. Buggs looked at me like he wanted to know the scoop but all I said was "Don't ask!"

Mom had dinner at the restaurant with the writer who wasn't totally bad news because he was a vegetarian and Mom told me the writer would like to write something about me because I was so different from most kids that a lot of people might not believe kids like me existed. Mom said he wanted to talk with me with a tape recorder and I said, "For how much?" and he said, "How much you want?" and I said, "We'll talk later," because I had an idea.

Then I went down to the field to the food stand and spoke to Mr. G. who's my boss. Every two weeks he comes to check on inventory and when he saw that sales were down on hot dogs and soda for my three nights a week for two weeks I tried to tell him people hadn't been showing up to the games because of all the rain and everything and he said, "We haven't had rain in three weeks, except once!" I just shrugged and said, "Who knows!" and then he said someone told him I was selling health food at his stand along with the regular American poison and I said, "Just almonds and juice." He said, "You keeping all the profits or what?" and I said, "I pay for the stuff, don't I?" He said it was cutting into his sales and that I'd either have to split the money with him fifty-fifty or else stop selling the food, so I said okay but I didn't plan on keeping very accurate figures because I had a family to support. I said, "Don't sweat the small stuff, Mr. G.," and he said, "And hot dog sales better be back up on your nights or else you're out." Then he paid me thirty bucks for my two weeks of six nights of work and I said, "Thank you, sir," and he said, "How you coming along in school, son?" I said, "Groovy, sir," and he said, "Don't piss away your education. It's important." I looked at my sneakers and said "GTF" and he asked what that meant and I said, "Gotta Think Fast." He looked at me like I was weird, so I said I had to split because I had a sex date. I took off leaving him to see what the stand needed and I rode Bicycle to Termina's and Buggs's and looked in the window and they were eating with their mother, who's dynamite-looking and lives with another woman who makes sculptures and talks deep. Termina's mother runs a bar on the main drag and Termina told me her mom and the sculpture lady are lovers, which Termina says is cool because love is supposed to be toward everyone and if they really love each other then people should mind their own business and I say "Right on" to that and it's better that two ladies are in love than having Mom getting nailed by a bunch of drunk guys who make me want to puke out my guts.

I went into the kitchen and Termina's Mom's name is Sorolta and she said, "Hello, you," and told me my skin was dry and I should eat avocados and camomile flowers. Then she asked me when I was born and I said Ides of March and she said, "A Pisces!" and I said, "A what?" and then Termina said her mom read astrological charts. Sorolta said I was a Pisces who are usually all fucked up emotionally and usually died young or went nuts from too much mental overload and that I should sleep a lot and I said, "Never fear—we're living in Eternal Mind," and Sorolta's lover, Avadi, said, "Amen." She was knitting something and seemed real quiet and nice and I said to Buggs, "I gotta talk with you, boy," so he got up from the table and Termina said, "What about me?" and I said, "Later, baby!" Avadi told me not to be sexist and I said, "I'm hip, not a dip!" She looked at me sideways and said, "Just don't be so precocious."

Buggs and me biked to Garrison Bight and watched the fishing boats come in. We saw two Egg Harbor types which Buggs thinks are the best and also three Uniflite jobs and even a Bertram and we waved to the skippers and they gave us their fog lights because it was getting dark. Buggs and I talked about being fishing guides when we grew up and we shook on it but then I remembered I'd probably be in New Zealand and got scared and stared at the water.

We drank piña colada drinks without rum on this houseboat where Buggs knew the bartender because he used to nail his mom before she decided to be a lesbo, so he served us good drinks and I saw the writer from The House drinking with this sexy woman with blond hair on the deck of the houseboat who was really smoking up a storm and eating shrimp. He didn't see me because Buggs and I were inside the houseboat and I figured this writer was a real smoothie and that Mom better be careful or else! I just stored that away in my vault and then I told Buggs I had a plan and that I'd pay him three bucks if he came down to the marina near Turtle Kraals probably on Thanksgiving Day and pretended to steal some fish from me. I told him it was only pretend because I only wanted him to fake hitting me and then ride away with the fish on the bicycle to a place where I would meet him later. I told him if he promised never to tell anyone about it I'd give him another five bucks and he said he'd do it for nothing less than ten because it sounded like I was up to some trick. So I thought about how much I could make and said, "Listen, I'll give you twenty-five bucks for the job. Ten before and the rest after, okay?" He said, "Deal me in!" and was so excited he went weird and shook my hand. Then we went back to his place and Termina was helping Avadi knitting. Avadi was toking on a J with headphones on and she was humming out loud and I looked at Termina and twirled my fingers and she nodded her head because her hands were tied in wool and she said, "Me and Coke are going skateboarding," and all Sorolta said was "Stay on the sidewalk." She smiled at me and said, "I bet you have Venus in your first house," and I laughed and blushed because I thought of Termina as Connie and me as Phil and it sounded like Sorolta had said, "I bet you have your penis in my daughter's mouth!"

Buggs said, "What time's Thanksgiving dinner on Thursday?" and Sorolta said, "We've been invited to The House for a Thanksgiving party," so me and Buggs were really happy and said, "Outta sight!" and Buggs said, "But what time?" and Sorolta said, "Stanley said after the football game's over on TV," so I said, "Probably five," which was good because the deal was at two at Queer Pier. I looked at Buggs and winked to let him know that everything would be cool for our little plan and he didn't have to worry about getting his fifteen bucks after the job was over.

Then Termina and me went out and Buggs winked at me and smiled like a sex fiend and Termina and me boarded down the block to the softball field. No games were on, so we went out by the fence in centerfield holding hands and Termina said, "Oh Phil!" and I said, "Oh Connie!" and then she showed me how to do it again, and pretty soon I caught on perfect because Termina's thighs squeezed my ears real tight and she sounded like she'd eaten too much and couldn't get enough air. She was moaning like crazy and then I thought I was going to suffocate, but she relaxed her legs and then it was quiet like when the tide has gone out and all the birds have gone out with it and there was only the sand. Termina said real low, "Oh-ho Phil-il!" and I said, "Don't mention it, Connie." Then she did it to me and my wang got hard like a rocket.

I got home to The House pretty late and Emmett was registering some people, so I sat on the front porch and chucked a rock to Leon and pretty soon Emmett came out to sit with me and smoke a cigarette. He said Mom wasn't home yet and I said she should be 'cause she wasn't nude dancing tonight and Emmett said, "Maybe she's got a date." I said, "Oh well, you know how it is with sex," and then I winked at him and said what Stanley always says about sex: "It's the strongest drive in the universe!" Emmett looked at me like he was suspicious and said, "What've you been up to?" and I said, "Sex is a private gig so I can't talk about it." He said, "Why's sex necessarily private?" and I said, "Why the hell you think they call your snake your privates?"

Then the writer and this woman with the blond hair pulled up in front in an orange Thing with the top down. They were smashed on something because they were trying to get a bicycle out of the back and couldn't get it together, so I got up and said, "Pro for hire," and the writer said, "We thank you, comrade," and he just left the bike hanging half in and half out of the car and went inside with the blonde. I had to shut off the headlights and Emmett said all creative people were fucked up. I took the bike and put it in the bike rack but I figured it would get ripped off because the blond lady didn't have a chain and lock, so I just left the bike in the rack and shook my head and said, "Sex'll do it to you every time!" I winked at Emmett and started yodeling until he got the picture and he said, "At *our* ages that's probably the only thing we can do!" and then we laughed and pointed at one another and I said, "How come everyone is a sex maniac at heart?" Emmett just sat there rocking on the porch looking sad and fat and smoking. He thought for a minute and then he said, "It's the only thing people know how to do to feel less lonely. People are lonesome creatures." I really didn't understand so I said, "Were you a sex maniac when you were young?" and he said, "I made the mistake of getting married." I said, "Can't married people be sex maniacs?" and he said, "Not with one another." I asked how come and he said, "Because people get bored with the same person. Sex is the only adventure left for most of us." I looked away and rocked back and forth thinking about Termina and wondering if I'd ever get bored playing Phil and Connie and I didn't think so, but Mom always says things are different when you're older and I'll find out soon enough so I shouldn't burn myself out thinking about it now because it will only get me down and I should enjoy being a kid while I still am one.

I went to the room and got my bubble jar and when I came out of the room I heard someone moaning. It sounded like Termina did and so I knew it must be the writer and the blonde playing Phil and Connie. I took a chair from my room and carried it over to the door and looked down the hall to the lobby to make sure nobody was around, and then I stood on the back of the chair, which was pretty dangerous and I almost tipped, but I grabbed the screen opening above the door and looked in and there was the writer and the blonde in the room with a candle burning. They were doing something the way I'd seen dogs do it and the bed was really creaking like crazy and pretty soon they were moaning away like mad and then they collapsed on the bed and the woman said, "Oh Jesus, oh fuck me, oh Jesus, oh fuck me," and I thought if Jesus could do that all the time I'd like to be a Christian starting last year. Then I got down real quiet and brought the chair back into the room. My wang was hard like a carrot and I figured it must be even better to stick *it* in than your tongue because Termina never said, "Oh Jesus" or anything really religious like that. I just went back to the porch and blew bubbles and I kept grumbling, "Oh Jesus, oh fuck me, oh Jesus, oh fuck me," and Emmett wanted to know where I'd heard that and I said, "A little nun told it to me." Emmett just looked at me and said, "You'll have trouble making a living in your life, I can see that."

The writer came out after a while and asked Emmett for some ice and I said, "I'll get it for him," and when I handed him the bucket I said, "Here you go, Jesus," but he was too eager to get back to the room and all he said was, "Bubble makers, I remember them," and walked back to his room.

Mom came back just as I was leaving the porch to go to bed and she was real high and seemed pretty happy and I said, "You'll have trouble if you live a long time. I can see it now." She said to Emmett, "Why's he still up?" and Emmett said, "Oh, what's the difference, Jody." Mom said, "I suppose he's old enough to know what's best for himself." She started down the hall telling me to get in bed like she hadn't even heard what she'd said about me knowing what was best for myself, so I figured her brain was pretty much dead for the night. I went after her and said, "He's with someone," and she said, "Who?" and I said, "Be cool, Mom, tomorrow's another day." She said, "You're too smart for my own good," and she came into the room and had a cigarette and pretty soon she was asleep and snoring, so I put out the butt and killed the light and pretty soon after that I could hear the Jesus stuff starting up again. I didn't know what to make of people, so all I did was say my own little prayer which goes "Dear God, another day, another zero, but I can dig it." Then I closed my eyes and the next thing I knew it was another day and I was glad too.

When I came back from school for lunch I saw the writer and the blonde coming out of the room and I told her her bicycle was still out front but it wasn't too cool to leave it there not locked up and she said, "What bicycle?" Then while I was still in ear range the blonde said, "I'd love to darling but I'm too sore," and she kissed the writer goodbye and he said, "Later," but it was different from the way Stanley used to say "Later" to women, which was "Later, baby," meaning *much* later.

Jetty told me he needed fish and that I should go out to *Tchandee* and pick them up and I said, "Gotta go tomorrow instead," because today was only Wednesday and he said, "What's the fuckin' problem with today?" and I said, "I'm busy today, okay?" He said, "Doin' fuckin' what?" and I said, "Ask me no questions . . ." and he said, "Listen, I'm fixin' fish for tomorrow because there's going to be a major freak show here after the ball game and I need time to garnish all the grub, you understand?" "I can get it first thing tomorrow," I said. "Snyder don't shrimp tomorrow, ass wipe," he said. "It's Thanksgiving, remember?" All I said was "I got rock pile after school so I can't help you."

"What!" Jetty seemed really pissed off.

"Rock pile."

"Fuck rock pile!"

"I gotta clean up the art rooms because Duchintow the Sow caught me chewing grape gum in the hall and she's allergic to it so I got rock pile for three hours helpin' the janitor."

"You'll go tonight then," he said.

I looked away and tried to think fast because I figured on me and Buggs working the switch on Thursday just before the sale and now I didn't know what to do. "I dunno," I said.

"Look," Jetty said, "don't start with me. Snyder shrimps at night anyhow. I'll give you six Js and two records, okay?"

"Why not just have him leave the fish on board in ice when he docks and I'll pick 'em up tomorrow?"

"Look, fuckhead! Try and get this straight. I gotta prepare food tonight, that's why. I'm doin' the bird and stuffing and salad tomorrow morning and the fish and yams and other shit tonight, you got that?"

"Okay, okay!"

"Just don't hand me rabbit turd and tell me it's jelly beans."

"Take it easy," I said. "It's cool." I had a plan now, so I felt okay again.

I talked to the writer before I went back to school. He was eating lunch reading a book, so I said if he'd take a run with me on Zodiac to pick up fish that I'd tell him all he wanted to know about me. He said, "Splendid. What time?" so I said, " 'Round seven," and he said, "I'll be drinking at the Pier House on the patio. Pick me up."

I rode Bicycle to school and told Buggs we had to change plans and that if he helped me I'd give him five more bucks and he said, "Definitely!" We played on the jungle gym and I told him he'd have to steal fish from me tonight and that we'd have to hide them overnight and that he'd have to deliver the fish tomorrow to Queer Pier where I'd meet him and he said, "No problem, boss!" We talked about where we'd hide the fish and we thought a long time and then Buggs smiled and said how about hiding the fish in the soda refrigerator at the food stand at the ball park. I said it'd be too dangerous, but he said nobody'd be there tomorrow and we could put the fish in late tonight because I had a key. I said it wasn't a bad idea because we didn't want the fish to rot overnight. Then I told Buggs the writer would be with me and that he'd be a witness so Buggs should wear a stocking or something over his head for a disguise and he said, "What if he comes after me and stops me?" and I said, "Good question." Then we figured we needed a witness but didn't want the witness to capture Buggs, so he said maybe we should get Cruz the crazy Cuban to help us because he had a switchblade his brother the boxer gave him. I said, "Great thinking!" and Buggs said I'd have to pay Cruz some money and I said, "Of course!"

We found Cruz beating someone up in the love tunnel by the tetherball pole right before the bell rang for afternoon to start and I told Cruz I'd give him five bucks if he helped me and Buggs steal some fish at the docks tonight and he said, "Shoe, why no!"

So I told him to wear something over his face and to bring his switchblade and to open it just once and tell anyone with me not to do anything stupid, and then Cruz said he wanted his money first but I said I wasn't stupid either and that after the job he should come to the stand at the softball field. Then Buggs and him made plans to meet at the Turtle Kraals at seven-thirty to wait for me because I said I'd be back with the fish at eight. Cruz asked why I wanted to have him and Buggs steal the fish from me and I said, "No can tell," like Charlie Chan and Buggs said to Cruz that since I was paying them to do this they weren't supposed to ask questions because if it was something bad then they wouldn't know about it and wouldn't get in trouble if it went wrong. I said, "Exactly!" and Cruz said, "You face 'zactly like a donkey butt!" All I said was "Just be there, Fidel!"

I stayed away from The House until six-thirty because I told Jetty I had rock pile. I went to Termina's house and we were alone because nobody was home. Buggs had to deliver newspapers and Sorolta had left a note saying she and Avadi were shopping, so Termina and me went in the back and played nudist colony by taking off our clothes and walking around like we were very rich. Termina talked in a British accent, saying, "By Jove it's hot!" and "I say old boy, wouldn't you rather kiss my buns!" and so pretty soon Termina was twiddling her thumbs and I said, "I say!" and she said, "What a jolly good day for a lay!" But we heard Sorolta come inside so we got dressed fast and went inside and Termina took me upstairs and showed me a training bra she said she had to wear for a couple of years so her tits grew in right and after that she was going to let them hang loose because she wanted to be honest about her body and not try to fake some guy out by being phony like people in the suburbs.

I ate tacos at Termina's with Sorolta and Avadi and Buggs and before I left I said to Buggs that I'd probably see him later and he said not unless he saw me first, which is how it was supposed to work out, so I said good luck and left on Bicycle for the Pier House where I found the writer and the blonde on the patio. Lights were on underwater beyond the patio and I could see lots of fish swimming in the lights in the blue water and the writer asked if the blonde could come along. I pretended I was Humphrey Bogart and said, "Who—Blondie here? Sure!" We went down to Curry's Dock and I had to use a flashlight to climb down into Zodiac and Blondie and the writer were a little loaded so when they got in Zodiac almost flipped over. Blondie screamed and I could see in the flashlight that she was pretty old, a lot older than the writer, but you can never tell when sex is involved, so all I said was, "Oh Jesus, watch your step!" like I was a skipper who wouldn't take any shit and Blondie said, "What an adorable little craft!"

I started the Evinrude on the first tug and really gunned her along with the flashlight guiding the way toward *Tchandee,* which had blue lights all around like Jetty said it would, and after a long time we got there and I must have told the writer my entire life story. He said he couldn't believe he'd forgotten his recorder but Blondie said she didn't think it would be good

to have me on tape and that the important thing was to just get
a feel for where my head was at and then use his imagination.
The writer just kept hitting this little bottle of booze he had in
his pocket.

When we reached the boat Snyder looked real pissed and
said, "It's about fuckin' time, me lad!" and just threw down the
fish and they landed on Blondie's lap and she started screaming,
"Get them off me! Just get them off, please!" We almost tipped
again and then the writer asked why I came out this far to get
these fish and I said, "That's nobody's business but my baby's."
Blondie got it together enough to say that someone was probably using me as a runner and she looked at me and winked and
I said, "No talking to the skipper while craft is in operation,"
and I sped off. She said something about how her old man used
to deal and always used kids like me to help him smuggle and
the writer said, "Jesus, that's it! Drug runner!" He started
laughing and telling Blondie he was going to write this story
about me that was going to be ridiculous, and I couldn't understand why anyone would be interested in my shitty little life.

Then we were back in a secret place at the Turtle Kraals and
I tied up Zodiac and we climbed the ladder that was slippery
on the first few rungs because the tide was out. Up on the dock
I looked around but didn't see anybody. It was real dark and
I led the way with the flashlight and just when we got near the
parking lot Buggs and Cruz jumped from behind a car wearing
pillowcases over their heads and pirate hats on top of them.
Cruz pointed his knife at me and said, "Geeme you feesh helse
I keel you!" so I handed them over saying, "Jus' take 'em, jus'
take 'em!" Blondie said, "Don't hurt him, please!" and the
writer said, "This is too fucking much!" and whipped out the
bottle of booze and took a hit. He was too loaded to be scared
or brave.

Buggs took the fish from Cruz and Cruz pulled me by the
arm and turned me around like in Life Saving and backed up

with me with the switchblade in the air above me saying, "No move, no hurt, can you deeg it?" and I said, "Take it easy, amigo," because I was a little worried Cruz would actually slice me up to be convincing. But he didn't and when they got to the bicycles Cruz pushed me away and I fell down to make it look good and then they rode off. Blondie and the writer ran and helped me up and they asked if I was okay and I said everything was cool. Then I said, "But Jetty's gonna be freaked about losing his fish."

We went back to The House and I told Jetty about what happened and Blondie and the writer told him the same thing and all Jetty said was "Cubans on bicycles with a blade? What the fuck is going on!" I said, "I'm just damn glad I'm not dead. What's some fish, right?" Jetty flipped and screamed, "Oh really! So what am I supposed to cook for tomorrow's meal— shit pies?" I could tell the way Blondie looked at the writer that she was hip to Jetty and Jetty just sat down and smoked a joint in the kitchen and tried to figure it out. He looked at me a couple of times suspiciously and shook his head and once he said, "Ya didn't know these guys did you?" and I said, " 'Course not. Jesus Christ, Jetty, whataya think I'm doin' anyway?" He said, "It's crazy. It's fucking crazy!"

I waited until Jetty was cutting up sweet potatoes and the writer and Blondie were gone and then I said I was splitting. Jetty was too stoned to care and was just making a whistling noise out his mouth and shaking his head. I rode Bicycle to the stand and Cruz and Buggs were there with the fish so I gave Cruz his money and said, *"Gracias,"* and he said, "Any time!" and counted his money. Then he looked at the money I stashed in my pocket and started to laugh. He took out his blade and opened it like he was real tough and said, "How much you life worse?" and I said, "Deal's a deal, potato peel." He said, "I only keeding you. I good, right? Marlon Brando!" Then he put his blade away and I said to him what Emmett says to me when I help him water the plants: "You do nice work, kid!" Cruz hopped on his bicycle and made a siren noise in his mouth and disappeared in the high grass of the field behind the ball park.

I unlocked the door of the stand and Buggs carried the fish in and we took out the Coke bottles from the cooler and put them on the floor. Then we put the fish in the cooler and closed it up. I gave Buggs his money and he said, "What are you doin' this for, Coke?" and I said, "You gotta grow up someday, right?" and I smiled at him like he should understand. He smiled back like he was hip, so I patted him on the shoulder and said, "Christ will The Worst ever be surprised at this!" and Buggs looked real confused, so I said, "You know what I mean! You know!" like I knew what I was talking about and it should be obvious, so Buggs started laughing along with me and said, "Right on, man. Right on!" Then we made plans to meet at the stand at noon tomorrow and get the fish so that he could take them where I told him to, and I said I'd give him another five and he agreed, so we put the Coke bottles on the counter by the cash register and I locked up the place. Then we rode through the tall grass and when we got to White Street we were covered with poor man's patches that stuck to our shirts like medals for a job well done.

Mom was dancing that night so I stayed at The House doing pogo stick in the street and once I bounced two hundred and six times before a lady in a blue truck almost ran over me. After that I just played it safe on the porch with Leon and looked at stars and pretended in my head I was from another planet and that the spaceship was coming to get me and Leon and take us home. Then Oakley and Kelley pulled up in the GTO that was all bashed in from the accident and smoking like it needed water in the radiator. They were laughing like fools as usual and when Oakley saw me she said, "Ma man Coke!" but I just took out my bubble jar and blew bubbles at them and said, "Who art thou?" and Kelley said, "Jump back!" and stared at me and licked her front teeth with her tongue. Oakley came over and asked me if I wanted to sit on her lap, which I thought might be far out because I could see her body underneath her shirt, but all I said was "Crazy Earthlings!" I blew bubbles at them and went to my room and locked myself in. I got into the sleeping bag and Leon slept beside me and way later when it was light out I heard Mom at the door. She left it open and smoked a cigarette there and I could see the blond guy who was going to buy all the coke from me standing at the door with her and it freaked me out, so I pretended I was asleep and Mom whispered, "He's ten going on five." Then I heard them kiss and I had to close my hands into fists because the sound bothered me so much. Then the door closed and Mom was looking at herself in the mirror and making kissing expressions and putting her hands in her hair like she wanted to look sexy. I peeked at the clock and saw it was almost seven and I thought about screaming my lungs out at her for being an all-night whore but then I thought about the big deal coming up and all the money I'd make and how I'd run away for good and go to New Zealand and teach her a lesson, so I didn't scream—only closed my eyes and tried not to worry.

Jetty asked me about the fish thieves again at lunch and Stanley and Snyder were with him and they kept asking me if I'd ever seen the guys before and I said, "They had masks on! Ask the writer and Blondie if you don't believe me!" Stanley said, "What about sneakers or pants? You remember anything like that?" I said, "It was totally dark out and they jumped us by surprise." Snyder said, "I told you to be careful, didn't I! Why didn't you fight them off?" He seemed real angry so I said, "What's the problem? It's only fish." Jetty said, like a volcano, "I knew this would happen. We should have hauled it one time directly." Snyder said, "What the hell you send him out at night for?" and Stanley said, "How'd the fuckin' Cubes find out he was carrying?" They all looked at me and I said, "Don't look at me!" and Jetty said, "Fuckin' Jorge won't let anyone cut in; he's got spies all over the key." I asked Jetty if it was okay for me to split and Jetty nodded and so did Stanley, so it was a majority. I split and as I was going Lewis was coming in looking filthy even before he'd washed one dish. He said, "Way to ruin our Thanksgiving, douche bag!" I said, "Wasn't my fault, porky pig!" and started to run. He couldn't catch me and all he said was, "You'll learn yours the hard way!"

I rode Bicycle to Queer Pier where guys in sunglasses laid six on a blanket large enough for three and I looked around for the drug dudes but they didn't show up. I figured it was too good to be true with Jetty faked out and easy money right in front of me and I just stared at the ocean and looked around for them. Around two I figured they'd chickened out, so I started riding away but then I heard this car horn beep and it was the two guys. I turned around and followed them to a parking place. They got out and the brown-haired guy said, "You got the goodies, Coke?" and I said, "You got the bread, Fred?" The blond guy said, "Seven hundred, right?" and I said, "Eight hundred, even Steven!" He said, "Oh yeah, sorry." So I said, "Let's see it," so he went into their car and took out an envelope and showed me a stack of fifty-dollar bills and I counted sixteen of them. I said, "Okay. Wait here. I'll be back." I started away on Bicycle and when I got around the corner I saw the blond guy walking into a phone booth beside the food stand and I got scared a second but figured I had to go through with it having gotten this far, but for a minute I had trouble breathing and wanted to cry.

When I got to the stand I saw Buggs waiting and he said, "You're late for a very important date!" I was breathless and said, "Sorry, sorry," and we went into the stand and got the fish and replaced the Coke bottles in the water that really reeked of the dead fish. The fish eyes were white-blue like ice cubes looked and I told Buggs that all he had to do was take these fish over to Queer Pier and give them to two guys who were in a yellow Fiat and that one guy had blond hair and the other brown hair and freckles and that they'd give him an envelope with money in it and that he should make sure to ask if all the money was there and if they said yes then he should make sure the envelope felt like it had about sixteen dollar bills in it and then he should split pronto and if everything went okay and he brought the envelope to South Beach where I'd be catching some rays I'd give him another twenty just as a bonus. He said, "I can dig it, boss!" Before he took off I handed him this note I'd written back at The House which read, "Goodies inside!" and told him to give it to one of the dudes. Then he took off with the fish in the basket of his bike.

I followed him down White Street a block behind to where we played Demolition Maniacs and then I followed him to Queer Pier and hid behind some shrubbery across the street from the parking lot. When I peeked through the shrubs I saw the yellow van from The House parked next to the yellow Fiat and then I saw Mom and Jetty and Stanley and Snyder standing with the blond and brown-haired dudes and Buggs was crying, saying, "Coke told me to. He told me!" and Jetty said, "This nice man called Jody, Mr. Buggs, to say he knew her son was trying to sell him stolen property and that we might be interested in checking it out." Buggs really cracked and said, "He bribed me, he gave me money!" I couldn't figure out what went wrong or what would happen and then I really couldn't believe it because Jetty was standing there with the fish in his hands and all at once the blond guy was holding a gun and so was the brown-haired guy and then three cop cars pulled into the lot with their sirens going. Jetty said, "Holy shit, a bust!" Then they were all being handcuffed and put into the cop cars and

Snyder was laughing and saying, "Be cool, folks, it's entrapment city!" Mom looked really scared and lonely and they wouldn't let her smoke and they put her in the cop car with Buggs. I could see she was crying and looked tired and really lost and small surrounded by all those men with guns who never did anything for her except buy her drinks and nail her.

I raced back to Emmett's house where he was sitting on the front porch with his shirt off and his face lifted to the sun. I ran up to him and he frowned and said, "Don't cry, Chris." I took one of his cigarettes and lit up even though I knew it was bad as shit for me. I told him the whole story and he just sat there for a few minutes and looked at his hands folded in his lap. He breathed real slow and said he was afraid something like this would happen sooner or later and it wasn't my fault but Jetty's and Stanley's and Snyder's, and then he went inside and called a lawyer and then the lawyer came over and Emmett and the lawyer talked to me a long time and finally the lawyer called the cops and made a deal with them to let Mom and Buggs free. Then Emmett and me and the lawyer went down to the station and Emmett made me coffee milk and the cops gave me a form to fill out. Now that it's all filled out the only thing I want to say is that I don't think people should get punished for being good capitalist pigs and supplying people with the stuff they demand in order to hang in there. Don't get me wrong because I'm no Ray the Gay, but I think the cops and Jetty and Stanley should listen to Emmett and just put their goddamn arms around one another and be cool till the world comes to its senses.

# SICKNESS

As I remember it, we were each excited that Friday with the expectation that my successful brother, Victor, would spend the weekend with us. At least I was excited and, to be exact, my name is Leo Judson Kannon, and I am thirty years old.

Now, if memory serves, I was living that month with my parents in their lovely new home that commanded, at least above the mulberry tree branches, a view of Manhattan Island. I believe my father once confided to me that the new home made him feel like a king, and I remember often wondering during that time to what position this assigned others, such as myself, for example, in his scheme of things.

I'm quite certain it was springtime. I so enjoy the springtime, and earlier that particular Friday morning, to give you an example, walking around the neighborhood, I noticed the smell of new grass for the first time in years. Also, I heard birds: a robin and a mockingbird. Frankly, their calling was so affecting that I fell to my knees and wept.

My younger brother's name, my successful brother's name, is Victor William Kannon. Without being invidious I should like to mention that my parents, though they call me Juddy, have never once called Victor Billy, or Vicky for that matter. I understand that I am quibbling here, which indicates, I suppose, that my title of fashion coordinator of Kannon Incorporated did little to assuage my sense of apostasy. (Surely apostasy might be too deprecating a term, and perhaps my parents' favorite phrase, "change of heart," or my wife's choice of "metamorphosis" is a more appropriate description. Yet even Joy speaks of her "daddy's sickness.")

But let me say just once again that it was Friday morning and that I had been awake since 3 A.M. The eastern wall of the room in which I was seated was completely glass. Dawn sunlight was pouring in, illuminating dust, and the room was all silence. I was alone, obviously, and could hear my heart clearly and distinctly racing toward my end. For an hour I stood, silently, thinking of my wife, Iris, and my daughter, Joy, sleeping in the apartment above the liquor store on West Eighty-third Street.

Victor, too, was on Manhattan Island that particular Friday. He was supposed to have signed a contract for his first book the preceding afternoon, but no one at the "Kannon residence," as the maid, Marie, always says, had heard a word from Victor, and so we were each uncertain about what had come of the signing.

My father, incidentally, Irving Isadore Kannon, is president of the Kannon Corporation and the major source, according to two psychiatrists, of my mother's migraine headaches. Indeed, one Sunday at the country club when my father was angry with me and my mother, Marion Helen Gilstock Kannon, he confided to me that when I was ill for six months (after I lost my acting job and wife and daughter), it was the corporation's money that came to my rescue, just as it had come to my mother's rescue on several occasions, and at several institutions, during the past ten years.

In any case, to the rear of the yard, to the east, beyond the pool and patio, stand several coppices of birch and hawthorne and mulberry trees. I was standing that Friday before these trees at my vegetable garden. It was a small garden, fifteen feet square, at which both my mother and I enjoyed looking, especially when we were relaxed on our prescription drugs.

As I recall, my father appeared at the back door that Friday morning. He is a handsome man, with thinning brown hair and blue eyes. He was standing in a bathrobe in the sunlight, and the angle of the sun had cast his large shadow onto the white wall behind him. Now that I think about it, I must say that I have always been terrified of my father.

"For God's sake, Juddy," he called out in an embarrassed whisper, "come indoors and put on some clothing."

I glanced at myself for a moment and said, "Why for God's sake!"

My father approached and wrapped me in my white cotton robe.

"Aren't you feeling well, Juddy?"

I gazed at him vacantly and smiled.

"Would you know who's on the mound today?" I asked.

He took hold of my shoulders and suddenly I wanted to cry.

"Let's you and I fetch the morning paper and find out!"

"They're playing Boston!" I burst out, delighted, and turning away, headed for the coppice of white birch.

"How silly, Juddy," my father called out, "when we have six bathrooms indoors!"

Nevertheless, I observed it soak the trunk and thought of something that happened between us years ago that never can be corrected.

After showering, I dressed in a cotton suit and tie and went to breakfast. My mother was awake, drinking coffee, smoking and reading the newspaper.

"How are you feeling, Juddy?" she inquired.

"Good morning, Mother," I said.

"Did you sleep well, dear?"

Before I could answer, my father stepped into the kitchen.

"Where are your shoes and socks?"

I glanced down, saw my toes, and made them spread open. Marie was instructed to locate my missing shoes and socks and when she returned, she held the shoes in the air and said, "I'm afraid he's deposited them in the commode again!"

I stood staring at the dripping shoes.

"That's funny," I said, and shook my head.

My mother's eyes brightened and her voice became musical.

"Sit down, Juddy, and have a fresh cigarette while I pour the coffee!"

My mother's name, incidentally, is Marion Helen Gilstock Kannon. She is a beautiful woman with wavy black hair and brown eyes. She is athletic, a better golfer than my father, and she makes an extraordinary eggplant parmigiana if she can restrain herself from throwing and breaking utensils and bowls. Ever since *Architectural Digest* expressed an interest in featuring the Kannon residence in next fall's renovated-home section, she has forgone her afternoon nap and now, occasionally, as on that particular morning, wakes before noon.

"What time is your appointment?" she asked me, setting down the coffee.

"Irv's scheduled several," I said. Irving Isadore Kannon is my father's name. My mother calls him I. "I and I are buying coats most of the day," I said.

My father returned to the kitchen with a pair of shoes for me to wear.

"I meant the doctor's appointment," my mother said.

"At three," I said.

"Would you prefer an earlier one?"

The sugar bowl dropped to the floor and shattered. I gazed out the window to where a gardening crew assaulted the lawn. Marie set about sweeping up the sugar and I apologized to her.

"Why were you outside without clothing this morning?" my father asked.

"Was that you, then, bellowing Shakespeare in the shower?" asked my mother.

I smoked down a cigarette, stared out the window, and

finished the coffee. My father left for conference with the sports section, and I put on his shoes and socks.

"So," my mother said innocently, "you're buying coats today?"

I directed my eyes to hers and smiled. "That's right," I whispered.

"You know, Juddy, your father and I have every confidence in you. You have such a natural artistic talent that I think you shall succeed at most any creative enterprise you undertake. Don't you, dear?"

The silence was replaced by the ignition of a gas-powered mower at the side of the house.

"What a lovely cup of coffee," I answered.

My mother cleared her throat and seemed hesitant to speak.

"If you're buying coats," she said tentatively, "I imagine you'll stop at Calvin Klein?"

"Either I will or I will," I said.

"Well then," she said brightly, "if you stop there, at Calvin Klein, I mean, tell me what you think of that tall blond model with the small mouth. She's the one with whom your father's been having an affair for years."

My father stepped into the kitchen.

"It smells as though the fan's not operating properly," my mother said.

My father looked at me expressionlessly.

"Care to take your little car today?"

My mother thought this unwise and immediately said so.

"With the tunnel and the traffic," she said, "the air will be insufferable. Take the Jaguar, Juddy."

We were backing from the driveway, my father and I, when Marion Helen Gilstock Kannon came running out in her housecoat, amidst the roar and fury of the gardening crew.

"I haven't any mozzarella for the eggplant!" She was breathless and put her hand to her chest to close her robe. "Victor won't have a word to say to me if I don't get mozzarella."

"All the better," my father said.

Still, my mother was in a panic.

"What am I supposed to do about this?" She looked past my father and our eyes met.

"You'll go to the market," my father told her imperiously.

"And what if I see someone? Then what?"

"You'll send Marie in the car."

The issue seemed successfully resolved, but my mother, Marion Helen Gilstock Kannon, buried her face in her desperate hands.

"Just go ahead," she murmured. "I'll think of something."

As I say, it was a lovely morning that particular Friday. The wind made a saving noise passing through the leaves of the trees.

On the way to Manhattan my father and I evaluated the Kannon Corporation's latest advertising motif: The Sensuous Spring! I refrained from smoking for a time, as I knew it distressed my father, but nearing the Lincoln Tunnel I could no longer endure without one. My father pulled into a gas station and I got out.

When I entered the men's room, I locked the door. It was a clean room with white tiles. I loosened my tie and lit the cigarette. I could hear traffic passing on the road. It was three minutes of nine. I studied myself in the mirror and then I closed my eyes and sank to my knees. When I was better it was five minutes past nine. I washed and dried my face, picked up the cigarette from the sink ledge, and opened the door to the sudden light.

At lunch I ordered a couple of very dry vodka martinis with three onions and ate a small salad. My father and I discussed Kannon's forthcoming fashion motif: Wonder and Warmth in Winter! It was May, and outside the street was bathed in sunlight. It brought back memories that aren't always helpful. My father made a phone call during coffee, and when he returned to the table he announced that we would split up for the afternoon. I was to visit Fairbrooke and order two hundred coats; he would make the Calvin Klein stop and meet me at the parking lot on Forty-first Street at quarter past four.

I rode the elevator to Fairbrooke, but I couldn't go in. I walked down the stairs to avoid Harris, the elevator attendant, and took a cab to the Pierre Hotel. I then walked across the street from the hotel, entered the park, and continued on to the small pavilion near the zoo. I stood in center stage, beneath the vault's constellation of profanities, and recited Act III, Scene I, of Hamlet. The sun slipped through the trees in beams of light and illuminated the audience that had gathered. When I finished the scene, several people applauded softly.

I remember standing in a doorway on the north side of West Eighty-third Street, in the shadows, staring across the way to the second-story windows of the corner building. I could see a figure sitting in sunlight at the dining room table beneath my favorite plant. From the windows, I recalled, you could see Morty making sandwiches behind the counter of the delicatessen. I walked across the street and into the lobby of the building. My name had been removed from the mailbox, and in its place, beneath the name Iris Anne Kannon, was affixed the name Terry Mahoney, whom I remembered as the photographer for the modeling agency that employed Iris. I considered going upstairs but realized I no longer possessed a key. As I was leaving, I heard my daughter, Joy, call out for something from her little room above the lobby.

I enjoy a nice walk, and walking to the doctor's office, I tried to remember the last time I had enjoyed one. I suppose my visit with the doctor was congenial. He offered me coffee before I began to sob inconsolably. Afterward I hailed a cab and returned to midtown.

I alighted from the cab at the same time as my father. I was behind him, and so he did not notice me. He leaned through the open rear window of the cab and kissed a tall blond woman. I crossed the street hurriedly to avoid embarrassing him and waited six minutes within the doorway of a church. I closed my eyes and raised my face to the sun. But I'm afraid that after a certain age the sun loses its magic.

To my disappointment, my brother was not at home to greet my father or me. Marie was watching television in the darkness of the living room. My father inquired after Mrs. Kannon while glancing at the headlines of the evening paper. Marie explained to him that Mrs. Kannon had been in bed all day. My father then announced he'd be drinking Gordon's with a twist of lemon, and I requested a double of the same. My father proceeded to walk to the intercom, and I noticed a small red light on the control panel glow dully in the darkened front hallway. He cleared his throat, said "I'm home!" and stepped into the bathroom.

Every Friday evening we eat sirloins, and my responsibility is to prepare the fire on the patio. Afterward I take a swim. I dived twice and swam the length of the pool. I was in poor shape and my muscles ached from the effort. When I returned to the barbecue to adjust the draft, I could see, through the den's wall of glass, my mother talking with my father. They both stopped when they saw me at the barbecue. I smiled. My mother came to the door with her hands on her hips.

"Feeling better?" I asked.

"Don't you think you should take off the suit before the chlorine ruins it?" she said.

I glanced down at myself and shook my head in dismay.

"All right," I apologized.

I felt better after the shower. It was hot and the towel I used was large and white and extraordinarily soft. It was a lovely towel, and I was thankful. I went to my room and looked out the windows. It was growing dark and the briquettes glowed a bright orange on the patio. The pool, full of lights, was blue, like an afternoon sky. I felt chilled before the open window, and for a moment I thought of my daughter, Joy, who is six and attends the movies on Friday nights. I leaned my head against the windowsill and recited the Lord's Prayer until my breath came back. By then it was completely dark and the breeze had died.

My father's voice issued from the intercom.

"Judd? We've company!"

I am afraid of so many things. I dressed carefully, however, and rehearsed a pleasant expression in the mirror. A man in sunglasses and long brown hair was seated on the sofa.

"Hello, Leo!" He rose and shook my hand, though I had wanted to embrace him.

"Can I get you an Old Times?" I asked nicely.

"Make it a double," he said.

"But you've just finished one," my mother protested.

"That's precisely why I want another," Victor replied.

Something inside me collapsed, but I poured two large drinks over ice, admiring the amber color. Victor was sitting on the sofa before the window and I brought him the drink. My father and mother were seated to the right and left of him, in blue suede chairs, and I sat facing him. Marie brought in a platter of cheese and crackers and set it before us on the coffee table.

"How nice," I said politely, but for some reason my brother winked at me.

My mother, meanwhile, was glancing over her shoulder at the bar.

"Did you finish that bottle, Juddy?"

"Yes, I did," I said gently.

"Why then you're drinking too much again."

"These things happen, Mother," I proclaimed, "when we can no longer love!"

My mother smiled sympathetically and averted her eyes.

"You're not an actor anymore, dear," she whispered.

A silence ensued in which I invented a tasteless joke which cheered me immeasurably, though no one seemed to understand its pertinence. The color drained from my father's face and he addressed me by gazing at my favorite brand of cheese on the platter.

"Victor and your mother and I were having a conversation on consideration a moment ago," he said. "I suggested that if Vic possessed proper manners, he would have phoned last night to allay our anxieties about the contract signing." He raised his face to my mother and nodded.

"That's all!" my mother said musically.

"I never mentioned phoning," Victor said. "The book had been accepted. The signing was just a formality."

"I believe what your father is trying to communicate," my mother said, trying to restrain an obvious impatience, "is that after burdening us with each and every one of your miseries, you might have had the consideration to share your joy with us."

"Share my joy!" Victor said incredulously. "But why?"

"Because we are your parents," my mother told him, "who have supported you through thick and thin."

"Supported me?" my brother said. "How?"

"We've given you household items," my mother said. "We've accepted Shawn, despite her religious background, into the family. And we've believed in you when you didn't believe in yourself."

Victor was amused. "How did you believe in me?" he said sardonically. "By suggesting I go into the fashion business and build a family empire with my so-called advertising wizardry!"

My father stood up to pour himself another drink.

"Let's not spoil the evening, Vic," he said cautiously.

My brother glanced at me and my mother noticed this collusion.

"Your father and I," she said derisively, "have difficulty understanding your generation. Because, you see, we were raised to be considerate of loved ones."

"That's true!" my father said from the bar. "Consideration has absolutely gone out of the world. You see it everywhere. People resisting their designated place in the scheme of things."

"Don't *you* talk to me about consideration!" Victor snapped, full of disgust.

A silence followed in which I, Leo Judson Kannon, heard my heart beat eleven times. My father looked to me for amplification and I raised my glass to demonstrate that it was still filled with bourbon.

"Of what are you accusing me?" my father asked Victor.

"You know goddamn well!" My successful brother turned away and gazed out the window.

I finished my drink and stood up, stumbling momentarily.

"Let me show you my side of the house, Vicky."

"Don't call me that!"

"Did you know that the silk wall covering in this room is padded?" I said. "Isn't it something!"

"Sit down, Juddy," my father said softly.

"I just want to say," I whispered, resuming my seat, "that not one of us understands what's important in life."

My mother glared at me.

"If your father doesn't understand what's important in life, Juddy, how do you explain the reality of this house and all the opportunities and advantages your father's money has afforded you two boys?"

"I'm sorry," I whispered.

"All single-minded compulsives," Victor answered, "do well in an epoch of economic boom."

My mother smiled meditatively and studied her nails.

"Ever since I can remember, Victor," she pronounced slowly, "your singular vindictive aspiration has been to destroy my marvelous family." She turned to my father and addressed him deliberately. "I refuse to tolerate any longer the presence of such a parricidal ingrate in my home."

My brother's head was bowed and, when he finally spoke, his voice was filled with regret.

"From whom do you suppose," he asked my father, "I have been receiving calls twice a week for the past six months requesting I ask my father about a tall blond woman he's been screwing for the last two years?"

"One sick and rancorous fabrication after another!" my mother screamed, and suddenly she was sobbing into her hands. I wanted to help my mother, but then I remembered how long it had been since such a thing had become impossible.

I suppose it is true that we live as alone as we die or dream. My mother stood slowly, with her face averted, and tried to affect great dignity. She then smiled peculiarly at me, said "Goodbye, dear," and walked gracefully from the room.

My father walked to the wide window and stared at the pool that was illuminated by blue underwater lights. The night was especially dark and clear. I finished my drink.

"This tall blond woman, as you call her," my father said wearily, his back to us, "is not a secret. Your mother knows all about her." He fell silent, staring at his reflection in the window. Then I could see that he was looking at our reflections in the glass. "I've known Marla since I was Juddy's age," he resumed. "We have lunch together once a week or so. I saw her today, for example."

"Did you have lunch with her today?" I asked, but then I remembered this would have been impossible, since I had lunched with my father.

"Your mother," he said laconically, "is unreasonably jealous."

"Why the hell shouldn't she be!" Victor said caustically.

My father turned to us from the window. There was something dead in his eyes.

"Because Marla is a lesbian."

My father turned to me and I smiled and lowered my eyes. I recalled how he had leaned through the cab window and languished there.

"Well," I sighed, "that settles that!"

Victor was now pouring himself a drink at the bar. My father observed him, waiting; but Victor ignored him.

"I have never done anything in this life for which my God would not forgive me," my father declared.

Victor raised his eyes and, gazing into the mirror above the bar, studied my father's image.

"Undoubtedly," my brother said, "your God must be an investment analyst from Hoboken."

I opened the door to the patio and inhaled deeply.

"The stars are twinkling for us again," I said, and then I stepped outside.

I was turning the steaks on the fire when Victor appeared at my side, smoking a joint.

"Why are you cooking your sandals?" he asked.

I glanced down.

"Why for God's sake!" I said softly.

My brother tried to reach for the steak fork, but I pulled my arm away. I stared into the briquettes. They were white and glowed orange.

"It doesn't help you to be around them," he said.

Marie brought the steaks to the patio and noticed my sandals cooking.

"Are you drunk, love?"

"I shall be fabulously drunk!" I promised.

She removed the sandals with the fork and placed the steaks on the grill.

"Don't flip them till I say ready." She smiled at me and returned indoors. Victor was smoking the joint toward the end of the patio.

"How can you stand being back here, Leo?"

I turned the steaks to be fair to both sides.

"Did I tell you she's living with another man?" I said calmly.

My brother was looking at the blue pool water.

"You can't blame her," he said. "Not after what you did to her."

"That's hardly any of your business!" And for a moment I lost control of myself. Afterward, I walked past my brother, retrieved the fork from the lawn, and went indoors.

At dinner we drank Burgundy with the eggplant, steak, and salad. It was a lovely dinner, but I ate very little. I can tell you this much about Hell: it will be a small hot room with spiders in the rafters; I shall be strapped to a chair and gagged, and through one small window I shall behold the first sunny day of spring, and not care.

"Things happen to us without our consent, don't they?" I said to my mother, smiling.

"I'm afraid you're drinking too much this evening, Juddy."

"You forget," my father chastised her, full of mocking affection, "that you're addressing the metropolitan area's most important fashion coordinator."

"That's right," I said, toasting myself.

My brother glowered at me and bowed his head.

"My brother is a talented actor," he said. "Don't either of you forget that!"

"Please pass the salt, Vicky," I said.

"Don't call me that!"

When he pushed me the salt, I said, "When you look back, Vicky, you only turn to salt."

Victor addressed my father.

"Why do you take such evident delight in seducing him with a vacuous merchandising career?"

My mother took the salt shaker from me and turned it right side up.

"I'm afraid your brother's envy is showing through," she told me, patting my hand.

"Your brother," my father told Victor, "happens to be an enormously gifted individual for whom acting is only one of many possible artistic avenues. If he has had a change of heart, then that's no one's business but Leo Kannon's."

"You behave," my mother said, addressing Victor, "as though you begrudge your brother the honor of being the vice-president of the largest independent women's retail chain in the state of New Jersey, the security of which, we must all acknowledge, has afforded you the luxury of writing your little stories and novels."

"The only thing I will acknowledge," Victor said, "is the imminent return of my brother to the hospital."

"You speak," my father said sharply, "as though we were responsible for the boy's sickness!"

We were all quiet. I counted my blessings. My father glanced to the chandelier and folded his hands on the table.

"I think everyone but Victor is prepared for dessert," he told my mother.

My brother stood from the table and, I noticed, his napkin fell to the floor.

"I will not allow you two to kill my brother," he whispered, and then he left the room.

"Well," I said ebulliently, after a moment, "I can't remember the last time we were all together."

My mother raised her face from her hands and addressed my father.

"It's because he loves his brother so very deeply, and has

always worshiped him so consummately, that he is denouncing us so very unjustly."

"I'm afraid," my father replied, addressing me, "that your brother is feeling guilty about his little writing coup in light of your change of heart and doesn't know what to do with himself. I suspect that your decision to shift artistic *emphasis* has made him feel unentitled to his category of artistic success. Unconsciously, I'm afraid, he's assigning to us the resentment he feels toward you for making him experience such acute guilt. In many ways I feel terribly sorry for him." My father winked at me and turned to my mother. "Ring for dessert now."

My mother swung a little silver bell above her wine glass.

"I want him to go away in the morning and leave us in peace." She took my hand and, patting it, wouldn't let go.

"Please pass the eggplant," I said, looking impatiently for it.

"Well," my father said, "we can't have him leave in the morning; I've arranged for the boys to see Shapiro tomorrow morning."

"Your lawyer," I said. "Why?"

"Because some things of a professional nature," my father said, "are best not discussed between a father and his sons."

"Please pass the goddamn eggplant!" I said furiously.

My mother signaled Marie on the bell once again.

"I've made the appointment for ten o'clock," my father told me.

"But Saturday is Juddy's morning to sleep in," my mother said.

"This is obviously more important," my father said.

"Screw the lawyer!" I said ecstatically.

"That's enough now, Juddy!" my mother scolded.

I reached across the table and lifted the carafe of wine and poured myself a full glass.

"The lawyer wants to discuss a tax problem with you boys," my father volunteered. "Don't be nervous."

I turned to my mother. "Am I still a boy?"

She handed me her lighter and I lit her cigarette.

"I'm afraid that to your mother and father," she said tenderly, "you always will be, dear."

After dinner my mother retired to her bedroom to watch television. My father remained in his study listening to Wagner and analyzing the latest computer report on quarterly sales. I'd seen the report the previous day and knew that sales in my exclusive department—sportswear—were off 6 percent. I poured myself a large cup of whiskey and coffee and sat on the back patio beneath a flood lamp, smoking and reading a book. It was a pleasant night, a sultry night, and I hurried indoors for another drink. Later I came across a passage in the book that interested me and committed it to memory. Then I set down the book and walked across the yard and into the darkness of the birch trees.

It was a lovely time of year. It was springtime. I turned to the house and observed my mother sitting on her round bed watching television and smoking a cigarette. It was such a very large room for one person, and I hoped the new carpeting and the canvas-padded walls would make it more pleasant for her.

I climbed the birch tree that overlooked the pool. The water was blue and transparent and I could see my father's initials, painted in navy blue, undulating gently from the white floor. It was a very large and clean pool. It was an immaculate and deep pool. It was the kind of pool that could break your heart.

I stood cautiously on the branch and recited the lines I'd memorized from the book. They were very pretty lines and I felt certain that the angels would stop to listen.

" 'Love cools,' " I whispered. " 'Friendship falls off, brothers divide: in cities, mutinies; in countries, discord; in palaces, treason; and the bond cracked between son and father. This villain of mine comes under the prediction; there's son against father: the king falls from bias of nature; there's father against child.

We have seen the best of our time: machinations, hollowness, treachery, and all ruinous disorders, follow us disquietly to our graves.' "

A bird deposited something on my shoulder and I climbed down.

When I woke in the morning I could hear the collar of the family dog jingling in the yard. I opened the expensive shutters and sunlight adhered at once. My father was driving wiffle golf balls from the edge of my little garden toward the pool. He was dressed in bright yellow pants and a red shirt that made me squint. Victor was collecting dog poopy with a hand spade.

"There's some more of it over there," I heard a voice say, and then I could see my mother, standing on the patio in a white tennis dress and wide-rimmed sunglasses, pointing to a spot in the yard. Her face seemed swollen.

My father drove two consecutive shots into the pool and glanced around to see if anyone had taken note of his accomplishment.

"You'd better remove your little balls from the pool right away," my mother told him. "I'm tired of them clogging the drain and ruining the filtration system."

She disappeared from view and then I could hear her requesting on the intercom that Marie bring her a fresh cup of hot coffee. I stepped into the hallway, pushed the patio button and spoke into the intercom.

" 'The Lord sent me to prophesy against this house . . . Now then, amend your ways and doings . . . The Lord will relent, He will withhold the evil He has pronounced against you. As for myself, I am in your power; you can do with me as you think right and good. Only be sure of this, that if you put me to death, you bring the guilt of innocent blood upon yourselves.' "

I returned to the bedroom window, leaned out, and waved to

everyone. My father was scooping out the wiffle balls with a small net connected to a long aluminum pole.

"Was that addressed to me?" my mother called up bitterly.

"How's the coffee?" I called out.

"Come down," she said gaily. "I'll open us a fresh package of cigarettes."

I bathed first. After I had raised myself to my knees, removed the mask and snorkel, and stepped from the tub to the medicine cabinet for my pills, I realized from the reflection in the mirror that I'd been bathing in my blue silk pajamas and slippers, and that my hair was covered with toothpaste.

My family was at the table eating breakfast when I stepped onto the patio. I fired my brother the football and it knocked over the pitcher of milk. My mother, Marion Helen Gilstock Kannon, employed her napkin to absorb the puddle.

"Isn't that your high school football helmet?" my father said, smiling.

I retrieved the football and returned.

"Go deep!" I motioned to Victor with my hand and faded back. A voice was racing in my head and I felt dizzy.

"Please take the helmet off and have some hot coffee," my mother said gently. "I'll have Marie bring you the cream."

I sat down. "Gorgeous morning!" I said and, removing the helmet, closed my eyes.

"Did you take your pills this morning?" my father asked.

"Pills, pills, the musical fruit," I intoned. "The more you take the more you ills!" I opened my eyes.

"And the less you wills," Victor said.

My father resumed reading the paper.

"Take them before visiting Shapiro," he said summarily.

"That's right," my brother said. "We're going to a professional this morning. No time for some schizo to embarrass the family."

My father peeked at me above the paper.

"Are you feeling out of register today?"

"I feel," I announced, "capable of engaging in fornication while leaping tall buildings with a single bound!"

"Speak with Shapiro and come right home," my father said. "Watch the ball game." He disappeared behind the sail of newsprint.

My mother was smiling at me.

"Pick up some nice imported cigarettes for yourself on the way home," she said cheerfully. "I'll treat you to them!"

Marie appeared with the cream and I sipped my coffee.

My father glanced at his watch and then at me.

"It's time you boys set out," he said laconically.

"How dandy it must be to live without emotions," Victor commented into space.

"I have emotions!" my father replied. "I just cannot afford to exercise them in a family where emotional excesses have done so much permanent damage."

"You never will understand the damage of your emotional detachment, dear," my mother said flatly. Her hand was shaking badly, as it usually does in the morning, and Victor helped her light her cigarette.

My father had stood from the table.

"Where are your pills, Juddy?" He was staring into the yard. "I'll get them for you."

"There are extras in the night table in my room," my mother said. She waited until my father was indoors before she turned to Victor. She was smiling, but her eyes were hateful, and I remembered the nightmares I had in which she was screaming at us.

"Until you apologize in writing to me and your father," she told my brother, "for your scandalous vilification of our lives, I positively refuse to allow you in my home. Do you understand me?"

Victor bowed his head.

"What I don't understand about you, Mother," he said dryly, "is how you can redecorate a house with a man more times in one year than you make love with him."

To my surprise, to my delight, my mother began to laugh. I began to laugh as well. It was a wonderful laugh, an emancipating laugh, and I wanted my mother and brother and me all to hug one another and pray together. But then my mother was shaking her head from side to side, and then I noticed she was weeping.

My father had returned to the patio and stood above us.

"What's happened!" He stared at Victor. "What did you say to her?"

"I was just saying," I said loudly, "that the worst day in my life was the day the sheepdog hanged herself in the yard. I'm sorry I said it, it's upset Mother, it's made her cry. If there's any way I can atone . . ."

My father resettled me in the chair and handed me the container of pills.

"Take two and shut your mouth," he said.

He moved to my mother and assisted her from the patio. She was murmuring something about mixed doubles at the country club.

"You just lay down," my father said. "The tennis can wait."

They started into the den through the glass door.

"You boys don't want to be late," our father said impatiently to us over his shoulder.

When we returned from the lawyer's office, my brother and I discovered our mother, Marion Helen Gilstock Kannon, crying in the den on the L-shaped sofa of cream-colored silk. My father was in the dining room, kneeling beside a newly delivered octagonal-shaped table of glass that was intended to replace the antique wooden one. He was examining the base of the table, wearing his reading glasses and golf outfit of yellow pants and red shirt. Marie was standing beside him.

"She's right," my father conceded. "The base is cracked. We'll have to return it first thing." He stood up with effort, pushing on a chair for support.

"It's a lovely table," I said. "A delightful artifact of prestige for the entire family to enjoy and the community to envy!"

For some reason my father ignored me. We trailed him into the den.

"I'm afraid you're right," he told our mother, who was sitting on the sofa with her legs tucked beneath her and dabbing her eyes with a little blue hankie. "You'll call the manufacturer Monday to have it picked up."

"That's preposterous," my mother snapped. "The table's come all the way from California."

"You will call the manufacturer first thing Monday," my father repeated.

"And what about the decorator?" my mother said, full of panic. "He'll want his thirty percent even though we don't want the table anymore. Because it's not at all right for the room. The proportion is wrong. It doesn't absorb window light or highlight the carpet as he promised it would."

"You'll pay him the thirty percent if need be," my father said.

"I will not pay Ira Flaming nine hundred dollars," my mother screamed, "for a table we are not going to take!" She closed her hands into little fists and struck her thighs. "I want to move from here, Irving! I despise this house. It bores me unspeakably. I want you to call the realtor in the morning."

My father glanced at the bar.

"You'll get over it," he ordered.

"I will not get over it!" And my mother screamed with such horrible conviction that my brother and father kept their eyes averted. Meanwhile, my mother turned to the window. None of us lives forever, and outside the window the sun emerged from a cloud and splashed light against the glass. I remember how the birds scattered abruptly and how I reached out to them.

"Don't assign the purchase of this house to me," my father said. "You were the one who inspected it first with the realtor. And Ira Flaming's designs were acceptable to you, not me. I've allowed you and your homosexual the privilege of doing whatever you thought best with this house."

"And I assign to you," my mother said with strange dispassion, "everything that is horrible and cold and hypocritical in my life!"

With this, my mother threw an ashtray at my father which went awry, smashed into the mirror of sunlight behind the bar, and sent glass exploding like a nova. My mother then rose and walked calmly from the room, her eyes luminous and vacant. A cloud drifted before the sun and the room fell into darkness, as if a fuse had blown.

I brushed shards of mirror from the bar top onto the floor and carried a tray of three glasses and a bottle of bourbon to the sofa. My father removed his eyeglasses and sat down.

"I've wasted my entire life working to gain the trust of people who resent and dishonor me," he said. "I'm sick of it."

Lightning cracked in a yellow scimitar above the trees, and then it began to rain with a loud announcement of thunder. I downed my shot with a swift backward tilt of my head.

"Pretend you're a cowboy at another time in another world," I suggested.

"Stop with that voice!" my father said.

"Think of Christmas in 1955!" I said.

"Please stop with that voice, Juddy!"

"All right," I said contritely.

"I don't mean to interrupt your bickering," Victor said,

glancing at his watch, "but I have arranged for Shawn to pick me up at three, and I do want to review our conversation with Shapiro with you."

"Yes," I said gently, "why did you think we'd refuse to accept the money? After all, it is in our name."

My father stiffened before the window of rain.

"I don't follow you," he said apprehensively. "Accept what money?"

"The twenty-five thousand a year that you've been hiding from us," Victor said. "The money that is in our name and legally ours."

"Shapiro seemed to think," I explained politely, "that you had kept the transfer a secret in the belief that we'd disapprove of the arrangement."

My father's face tightened.

"That's not what I wanted Shapiro to discuss with you boys," he said impatiently. "The issue was whether you'd be willing to loan that money back to the corporation. I only wanted you boys to believe—"

"Believe what!" Victor said. "Another one of your so-called mistakes in judgment?"

"If you'd shut up a moment and allow me to explain," my father said, and he turned shamefully to me. I lowered my eyes. "I didn't tell you boys about the stock transfer to your names because I feared, quite frankly, that it would be psychologically damaging for you to know you had so much money at your disposal." He cleared his throat. "Now, of course when Shapiro told me this was illegal I had him tell you the truth according to the demands of the law."

"How reassuring," Victor said, "that a lawyer can coerce a father into telling his sons the truth."

"I was not coerced," my father said emphatically. "Long ago I wanted to place this money directly into my estate for you boys, but the taxes made it prohibitive. Placing the corporation in your names and then depositing funds for you was the most practical legal alternative."

"If you've put the money away for us," my brother said, "then I assume there is a bank account in each of our names, and that you will show us the records of such accounts."

My father smiled superciliously.

"It would be more correct to say that the corporation owes you boys money. The capital is largely in nonliquid assets."

"Why the hell do you pretend," Victor said contemptuously, "that you left the money out of your estate for tax purposes when in fact you kept it out because you didn't want to relinquish control of it?"

"If I've used that money to pay my creditors," my father interjected, "there's no reason to think I won't restore the funds when the economy recovers a bit."

"The simple truth," Victor said, "is that you kept the transfer secret from us not because you thought its disclosure would have a negative effect on us, but because you wanted to keep the money for yourself—to employ it as you wanted. You couldn't stand to give it either to the government or to us—so you cheated both by acquiring tax advantages in our name and then keeping it secret so you could embezzle the money."

My father shook his head incredulously. "Sickness!" he said.

"Then show me the official accounts of how much you owe us," Victor persisted.

"I'll have Shapiro present you our records the middle of the week."

"Oh hell," Victor said, full of disgust, "I won't be sullied by your money. I just want you to admit your crime against your sons."

"The only crime," my father said calmly, "exists in your own mind."

There was a silence in which I watched clouds sail away beyond the window.

"About the money that is now legally in our name," I said nicely. "When will we receive it?"

For some reason my father smiled; it was the type of smile that revealed discomfort.

"You will each receive twenty-five thousand dollars a year from the corporation. But, as I say, what Shapiro was supposed to discuss with you boys was not whether you'd accept the money, but whether you'd feel any compunction about leaving the money with the corporation so that it might reinvest the profits as it sees fit."

Victor laughed derisively and turned to me. "You see!"

"I'd prefer to have the money for my own use," I told my father.

My brother frowned. "You're not actually going to accept this man's money, Leo?"

"Oh yes," I said softly. "Then I'm leaving for a long vacation before starting over again." I wanted to look at my father but couldn't.

My brother's face was full of pain.

"So Leo Kannon has become just another dirty pharisee!"

"Don't say that to me, Vicky," I said gently.

"Just another dirty onerous pharisee!" he said again.

As I remember it, Victor started into the living room and I pursued him. The living room was long and sunken and ended at a wide convex wall of windows which faced the pool. I leapt the sofa and caught my brother at the piano. I punched his face and he dropped to his knees. He put his hand to his face and stood up.

"Pharisee!"

He was amorphous from the tears in my eyes and I said, "Shut up now!" And then, as I remember it, I punched my brother repeatedly, crying out, and he fell backward into the piano. The top slammed down and my mother's favorite glass piece, "A Bird in Flight," exploded at once, as if shot. I could hear my mother screaming over the intercom, "This is my house! This is my house!" and then my father stepped between Victor and me.

My father seemed smaller and more vulnerable than I'd ever seen him, and I knew—I just knew—that I could have floored him if I'd wanted to.

"Please, Leo," he said, and escorted me into a chair. "Don't do this to yourself," he said weakly.

"Very well," I said calmly, smiling. I glanced at the knuckles of my right hand and saw that they were bleeding.

Marion Helen Gilstock Kannon stood before us in a green bathrobe. She was stunned at the sight of the broken bird and dropped to her knees to examine the shattered glass.

"Who's responsible for this?" she whispered.

"It's just a heartless piece of glass," my brother said, bleeding from his face beneath the piano.

My mother could not remove her eyes from the shattered glass, which she held in her hands. She attempted, twice, to stand, and then, still on her knees, covered her face in her hands.

"I feel so inestimably sorry for you," she muttered. "I so very much pity you your life."

Then she managed to stand and walk from the room. When she reached the three steps that rose to the marble foyer, she turned, rigid as a statue, and said, "I shall never forgive you for what you have done to me." She seemed to address us all. Then she drifted away, to the northern side of the house, where she lived alone in her padded room.

I stood in my room, staring out the western window. I watched my brother load his suitcase into the red car. Shawn, his confrere, as he called her, was sitting on the hood of the car, staring at Victor. When they entered the car, Victor slid across the seat to allow Shawn to drive. I waved as they passed the window, but apparently neither of them saw me.

My room was so very large. I walked across it, remembering the Christmas of 1955 when my mother wept on the stairwell of our first home after her father had shot himself, and glanced out the eastern window. My mother was now sitting by the pool in the late afternoon sun, and one bird was singing. She was wearing sunglasses, reading the paper, and smoking a cigarette. Marie was mixing her a drink. My father was driving wiffle golf balls into the pool.

To the south I could see Manhattan showing above the mulberry branches like a series of tombstones. Sunlight burned portentously in the upper windows of the World Trade Center, and the overhanging roof above my room cast a dark shadow before the window so that I could see my image floating translucently before me. I picked up the phone and dialed carefully. My eyes closed and my throat contracted when I heard Joy say hello. It had been nearly a year.

"Hello, darling," I whispered. "Remember your De-da?"

Joy's voice, however, was part of a recording that continued without me.

". . . my mother and I have gone for a walk in the park and will return shortly. Please leave your message when you hear the funny tone."

In the background I heard the recorded voice of my estranged wife, Iris, say, "What are you doing with Leonard's machine, Joy?"

When the cuckoo signaled and it came my turn to speak, I sat on the bed and stared out the window. I remember that rain water was purling along the roof gutters and that the sky imploded through the window like a first breath. When the cuckoo sounded again, intoning "Cuckoo! Cuckoo! Cuckoo!" I knew my time was up.

It was Saturday, May the fifth, at 3:51, to be exact. I would go back to that place, for a second time, the next day.

# LIFETIME

## FIRST DAY

DAY

Springtime wasn't two weeks old when *they* announced that two hundred and seventy-three miles south of Mahoney's absorbent glandular system a goddamn nuclear power plant threatened to blow its lid of strontium 90, cesium 134, cobalt 60, and iodine 131. Of course, the experts were cool as cucumbers, but the local milk cows had lined up at the fences, staring south, and wouldn't eat their chemicalized breakfast fibers.

Mahoney lay there in his sheetless bed wondering how much longer he could continue his quotidian ritual of rising and shining on a steady diet of dwindling enthusiasms. Still, when the phone rang, he committed himself to one more day by moving his eyes from the ceiling, reaching above the blankets, and answering to Olive, the twenty-year-old sleaze queen who preferred flushing her children down the toilet to the nuisance of contraception.

"Ah'm earnestly awaitin' the arrival of yore five-speed, dearie."

A breeze flung the white mesh of curtains into his face, and outside the window, through the early morning lake fog, Mahoney could see Judith Chapters, his last hope, collecting bits and pieces of wreckage on the beach. His voice percolated hoarsely with sleep and Olive didn't seem to understand. Like most of the benighted, however, she reflexively skipped over a good deal.

"Seven-thurty and my rod and staff is still in baid?"

Something flared outside the window and Mahoney's eyes rolled into his head for asylum. The sun had ricocheted off the lake like a scream, and disappeared again as quickly. Mahoney sat up, holding his temples in his hands. He inclined his forehead on his device, or so it seemed, and inquired of Olive if he'd been, well, drinking again.

"Wail, after you jettied din-din on the bar, cupcake, you freshened up outdoors in a puddle of curb water. Don't we 'member that? 'Cause by the time I had things tidied up, you wasn't there no more."

Mahoney vaguely recollected Judith Chapters retrieving him from the gutter. On the other hand, he couldn't remember what had transpired after she'd set him down in her back seat. He advised Olive to check back at twilight.

"And just what am ah supposed to do with my urgency till thain?"

Mahoney suggested she multiply and be fruitful with herself, and Olive surely didn't care for someone telling her to go do it to herself.

Downstairs, Mahoney discovered that Judith Chapters had left a note beside her blue pail of lake flotsam on the kitchen table; he peeked out the window in time to see her Volvo catapulting dust as it streaked away.

Dearest:

When I checked your pulse this morning, you were on your side, smiling and embracing the pillow. I must confess it was splendid to learn of your affection for me last night. Who knows just what will happen with my egregious life with John Hancock! Unfortunately, I suspect you are no more suitable a gentleman than he, and last night you beset me with the eyes of an incurable nympholept. Now, seeing as I've been scorched by your expectant type since Napoleon was a cadet, I'm afraid it will be best if we limit our visits to The Cafe.

Meanwhile, I'm leaving my friends a list of vitamin supplements to protect against the Three Mile Island fallout. Please keep in mind that this is hardly a propitious time to go exposing one's gender to our tragic atmosphere.

Now, *do this*! Take:

1 to 2 tsp. of kelp per day.
1 to 2 tsp. of lecithin per day.
2 to 3 tsp. of Brewer's yeast per day.
25 mg. of B 1.
100 mg. of B 15.
3,000 mg. of vitamin C per day.
600 IU of vitamin E per day.
1,000 mg. of calcium per day.
500 mg. of magnesium per day.

*Ciao* now, JC

The dogs began barking at the sound of Mahoney's boots and he let all twelve into the run. The lake frothed with whitecaps from the north wind and it hardly seemed like the season of resurrections. Mahoney just happened to be musing leeward of the coffee pot, so by the time he'd hosed down the menagerie, the pot had blown its little glass lid in the kitchen and the stove was covered with El Exigente's profiteering finest. He scrubbed it all up and started over again. Then the phone rang. He lit the Chesterfield and made it through the doorframe on his third go.

"This the humane officer or what?"

"Speaking."

"Well, we got us a dead dog out on back. Boy kilt it chasin' deers. Wants to know can he mount the head for hisself?"

"No ma'am."

"Why then you get your ball o' wax out here quicker'n Jack B. Nimble else my boy can use that head."

The phone hummed a special hangover tune when the line went dead. Mahoney called Chaney at the sheriff's department to suggest a cruiser be sent pronto.

"Finally got hold of your dirty book!"

"Listen up, Chaney."

"What hell kinda title is *Picnic in Panty Park*?"

"Damn you, Chaney! Listen up!"

"Don't tell me you do that sort of smut in real life?"

Mahoney told him about the dog and hung up. The goddamn coffee was burning again and he needed more milk than usual to set the taste right. Afterward he fed the twelve dogs in one trough in the windowless room where the state said he had to use the gas every ninety-six hours. Mahoney was closer to thirty than he'd ever been before, yet when it was bad like this, he kept hearing Mom calling him to breakfast. He peered through the door of the ghoulish room and imagined what it would be like to use the gas on them. Surely he was guilty of his share of transgressions, but he'd never be accused of execution. He was the thrifty type, and liked to save what he could. For some reason, this seemed to exclude, or at least not include, himself.

Why it should feel *so* good for the male to turn his back once he'd stuck it in intrigued Mahoney. He had the kind of mind that was no less transfixed by canine tail-to-tail recreation than it was by, say, a total eclipse of the sun. He stood watching with folded arms. The male's lubricous weeny nosed from its sheath and made the crowd of children point and giggle.

The bitch was registered. Mahoney took her home to the inscribed address and collected a cash fine of ten dollars for lunch money. Chaney then radioed on the CB to say that a headless dog was in a baggy in Mahoney's garage. Mahoney reminded Chaney of the importance of suppressing atrocities before lunch hour; then he headed for The Cafe and Judith Chapters.

Judith was weeping in the kitchen. At first Mahoney figured onions.

"Judith?"

"This too shall pass."

Phyllis walked in with five orders and Mahoney said, "Judith will be right back."

"This will certainly piss off the tippers!"

Mahoney let her know that the world was coming to an end.

"All the more reason to hurry along the omelets, Mahoney!"

"Pray for perspective, Phyllis."

"Fuck off!"

"God bless."

Outside, it had turned blustery and radioactive. The wind had shifted and the sky was a cobalt dome scooting south to north. The robins hadn't shown up for spring yet, and the prodigious migration of geese had dwindled to nothing. This, the mayor announced, signified nothing pertinent to the community; of course he was overweight and a former gas station owner who advocated the proliferation of highways.

Judith had been fasting to protest what specieists called "the seasonal baby seal harvest," and Mahoney couldn't help but believe that her mournful display of tears signaled a protein drain.

"If you'd just take a yogurt and—"

"No talking!"

She remained half a step in front of Mahoney, who took in this fragile woman's full length of legs in silence. Her long blond hair was lambent with neglect and flapped about in the breeze. The pink day-old flowers behind her ears were wilted now and didn't stand a chance in the breeze; they blew away, one petal at a time, and to Mahoney it seemed futile to run into traffic for the missing pieces. At the end of the block Judith sighed and confronted him with her bleary green eyes, infamous for those floating pieces of ocher.

"I'm okay." She nodded hopefully and they started back. Mahoney held her hand and watched the wind bring the color back to her face. By the time they had stepped into the kitchen she was crying again, and the orders were stacking up. The twelve o'clock news reported that despite the possible evacuation of one million citizens from the Harrisburg area, the First Lady would not cancel her fizzy christening of a Trident submarine.

"If it melts down," Judith said, "I'm fleeing. My belongings are packed."

Where, Mahoney wanted to know.

Judith hoisted a glass of juice to her lips; from the looks of those dancing pits Mahoney guessed grapefruit.

"Cleveland," she said.

This irony was an encouraging sign and cheered Mahoney so very much that he thought he might be able to postpone his drinking until after lunch.

"Is it safe to fast during nuclear assault, Judith?"

"I cannot allow myself to forget those baby seals. Or the boat people."

Judith threw parsley on two omelets and told Mahoney to butter the whole-wheat bread. He, in turn, asked if juice fasting ever resurrected the bludgeoned or eternally fucked over, and the kitchen was suddenly as cold as a mortuary.

"I don't need your dreary antipathy now!" She ladled six bowls of soup and decorated them with what the menu called a "dollop of sour cream."

"Will you come for dinner, Judith?"

"*I am fasting, sir!*"

"To watch *me,* then?"

They stood side by side now, squinting at the green order slips clipped above the counter. Judith said, "Don't pretend you don't have plenty of others," and handed him a bowl. Mahoney set to work scooping marinated vegetable salad.

"The others mean nothing," Mahoney whispered. "Absolutely nothing."

She turned her sorrowful eyes of shattered ocher upon him.
"Nothing," he promised. "Nothing."

Flakes of snow appeared suddenly behind Judith and stuck to the windowpane. "I'm thirty-seven with two ex-husbands and an alcoholic lover I don't know what to do with. You certainly don't need the likes of me."

"I am all alone in this world, Judith."

"You're just hungry, dear."

The sandwich she pushed before him generated memories of Mom in the days she was capable of slicing such things as cheese and bread without getting her wrists in the way. Judith was right. Mahoney filled his face with lettuce and tomato and didn't feel as close to the end anymore.

Judith tapped the bell for Phyllis to pick up, and all their work went out the glassless window in a blink of the eye.

Mahoney identified the headless dog from its tags and notified its owner, who said he hadn't seen it in three months anyhow, so Mahoney hung up and incinerated Skippy. He watched the ashes plume from the chimney and over the lake, and wondered if John Hancock would willingly step into the flames if Mahoney asked him politely.

NIGHT

Olive had the boilermaker set up and Mahoney got busy. After the second chaser had rubbed out the requisite number of brain cells to ignite that reprobate buzz of peace, Mahoney found Elaine's—that is, his ex's—importunate ghost beside him at the mahogany counter. This was not good. He scooted around the block with her to get something straight, insisting that all ghosts must relinquish their strangle hold on the heart after a year's absence. But Elaine wanted to know why blessings were only the embryo of curses and Mahoney didn't have an acceptable answer. He just said the usual about three years down the tubes, he supposed. So Elaine came back inside and supervised his drunk. It took the better part of a ten-spot to send her back into the ether.

Olive certainly was a revelation in her transparent white blouse. Well, at least a sight for sore eyes. She didn't seem right amiable, though, and Mahoney's inquiry enkindled her wrong end.

"Just pipe down, snotrag!"

What's more, the evening paper was filled with the annunciations of the necrophilic. The HEW secretary's insouciant claim that no one would die in Harrisburg seemed as gratuitous as his ardent crusade to prohibit smoking on airplanes, which themselves kept falling out of the sky with disquieting regularity. And on page 2 James Schlesinger, capable of generating all the sympathy accorded an indicted war criminal, was advocating acceleration of the licensing procedure for nuclear utilities. Mahoney wondered why the paper failed to mention his former chairmanship of the homophobic Atomic Energy Commission.

"Whyn't you just drink up 'fore you go wacko?" Olive said, and Mahoney conceded publicly that, after all, there was next to nothing one could do about those plutocrats whose heads were engorged in their complicitous industrial duodenums. It all helped Mahoney understand why he wanted only to save the dogs from the gas and write pornography for the irradiated masses. Still, the price one paid for such political surrender registered as a slight burning in the heart—as if from a butter knife stabbing.

Then Mahoney, remembering how the moron made time fly by hurling the alarm clock out the window, felt entitled to speed things up by soliloquizing in the urinal. Before he knew it, Olive entered to announce closing time.

"And just who you suppose gunna mop that up?" She pointed at Mahoney's feet.

"Won't flush!" Mahoney pumped the little chrome phallus to prove that the overflow was indeed a collective endeavor.

Olive's genuflection seemed depraved, considering the floor, and her ejaculation "Oh my!" even more so. But when she recommended Mahoney's place, he figured this was positively copacetic with whomever he might be at that moment.

Alas, Olive's live-in, Harold, the minister's boy, was waiting out front in the '59 Cadillac with an invitation to hamburgers and fries, and Olive asked in her inimitable point-blank candor whether Mahoney would be gentle or a typical roughhouse pervert. Whatever the lady wanted, he said, and the twenty-year-old Cadoo acted half its age and peeled rubber a hundred yards up the hill without them. The town's drunken canaille expressed their amusement in wild applause, and not even the silent cataract of fallout could distract Mahoney from fantasies of his imminent ingestion.

Now, Olive was the woman who flushed her children down the toilet because the pill made her fat, the IUD generated infections, and diaphragms and rubbers just plain sucked. For his part, Mahoney questioned the advisability of the rhythm method for zero population growth. Providentially, though, Mahoney's abstention from the more traditional expression of high lust contributed to the discovery of a more piquant alternative. The batteries of Olive's aid gave way near the end of their acrobatic sodomy, so Mahoney assigned his hand to her darkness; and when Olive's owl-like tremolo reached crescendo, Mahoney hurried things along on that girlishly tight forbidden side. He could feel the contractions just enough to bring them off together in a happy fruition of collapse.

Mahoney wasn't making reservations for Heaven.

## SECOND DAY

**DAY**

Nikki phoned at four-thirty that morning to ask if Mahoney had forgotten about her. The note beside him said Olive had gone home on all fours; Mahoney, more socially discreet, remembered to step into his pants before starting off. When he parked before the terminal half an hour later, a porter seated on a luggage cart asked if he was Mahoney. The humane officer confessed he wasn't proud of the fact, and the porter said the lady had took herself a cab.

Mahoney bought coffee on the way home from the airport and sat in the doggy van with the side door open to the east. The sun rose once again, and he felt all the enthusiasm and splendor of stepping into a wet jockstrap. He acknowledged that evanescent attachments of the flesh wouldn't keep his home fire burning very far into the next decade, but without them there seemed to be only insomnia and loneliness; that is, nothing.

Mahoney stared at the cold purple horizon. He sought a landlord with properties somewhere over the rainbow.

The first shirtless day of spring, and below him the boy cried, "Strontium 90, cesium 134, iodine 131, ready—hike!" The pass went for a touchdown and Mahoney remembered how his dead brother and he could once whip any of them.

Mahoney, however, had lost the winner's touch: no amount

of cajoling or saucers of milk could get the pussy to step from the concrete crotch. Still, the "Roving Reporter" thought a picture of Mahoney with outstretched arms at the summit of Mrs. Dexter's aluminum ladder would amuse the citizenry; so Mahoney smoked three Chesterfields seven rungs up, waiting for the photographer to rove over. Surely this ludicrous photo would not ignite hope in the innumerable homes of the abject, but Mahoney allowed that these little charades were necessary distractions from more serious crimes, such as child abuse and the viewing of televised athletics. The point is Mahoney did what he could to help. Come Judgment Day it might score points, or at least subtract demerits.

It was one of those days. Fallout wasn't exactly what the doctor ordered. Mahoney told Chaney where he could be reached and headed for The Last Stop. A couple of shots of Wild Turkey sat waiting on the bar top, and Mahoney looked heavenward twice. There were only Olive and he at one o'clock, and Olive was darning a headcover for Harold's driver. When she rang up his tab, she walked like the first morning after your first all-day horsy ride.

"The price ah do pay for your kinkiness." Olive sounded more sad than hateful; she just assumed she had to be a victim if she was ever to belong to a man.

Mahoney remembered the Boy Scouts. "You seemed alert and eager to learn."

"Ah'm not denying ah wuzn't!"

Chaney called to report a fight between a raccoon and a terrier on the corner of Hoot and Holler. He had to go. Sure, he was always running out on her; but there wasn't any peace, anywhere.

The man told Mahoney his name was Joe, and Joe wondered why the mayor would permit a longhair to be the humane officer. Mahoney and he agreed that the times left you cloying from its inaccessibility. Joe stood there with the hose on the carcass and when Mahoney asked him why, he said, "God-damn flies, boy!" Mahoney shoveled the coon into a brown trash bag and reminded himself that goodness and mercy were obvious only to the omniscient, which meant he wasn't the only one hopelessly stupefied.

The Irish terrier was tied to the garage door. The tidy disap-pearance of the raccoon left him nonplused—as though this suddenly questioned the necessity of an instinct that led to such an anticlimax.

"Balls for brains," Joe said. His eyes were small and black, and he was missing teeth between his lower incisors. Joe was just another citizen with little else to do but bore the hell out of Mahoney with another doggy biography. But the times re-quire that we pretend we haven't seen one another on those Saturday morning cartoons *they* have rerun for twenty years now. Mahoney knew we all had to walk around in it; and he was polite, all ears and attentive eyes.

"Snapped the neck in three shakes," Joe said. "Broke his chain and went right for them cans. Doughnuts is what it was. Larry's a good boy, but he belongs on the farm. Sure does love them doughnuts." Joe moved Larry sideways and the terrier went to bite the hand that fed him. "See them lines? That's a ratter's stance." Joe winked at Mahoney and looked into the trees. "Larry's had a good life. He's two now. But you can't keep a ratter off the farm. No, a ratter's got to run it outta himself. Otherwise they get into the cans, make a mess of things. I'll ask Doc to put him away tonight."

Scrutinizing Joe, Mahoney understood why, at twenty-nine, he was at his happiest five shots to the wind on the northern-most stool at The Last Stop.

NIGHT

Judith wasn't at The Cafe at dinnertime and Mahoney couldn't reach her at home. He was sitting on the savings bank wall when she pedaled past on her bicycle in a Yankees hat and sunglasses. He hadn't seen her in thirty hours and the new register of his heartbeat betrayed his conviction that all he wanted after the catastrophe with Elaine was a few years of loneliness. Judith's legs were bare beneath her little pink jacket and he felt a jealousy amounting to heartbreak on witnessing this publicity of thighs. Her brakes screeched in recognition and she circled back to him. In fact her pants were missing; her panties were green with little blue stars.

"Must you stare!"

She was in a fuss, and Mahoney's eyes filled with question marks.

"I was sitting quietly by the water cooler in the library, researching the crimes of the Nuclear Regulatory Commission, when one John Hancock appeared with a jug of wine and created a scene, which ended in the street with his ripping away my drawstring and pants. I have fled on my bicycle."

"I'm sorry, Judith."

"I am devastated!"

"No need to cry."

"I am just *so* angry!"

Mahoney hoped his arms would help her get over it.

"This John Hancock is the man you live with?" he whispered.

"Not anymore!"

"Judith?"

"Will you help me move out tonight?"

"Only because I think it will be best for you."

"I'll go to Phyllis's for now."

"Judith?"

"I really must get some pants on."

"All right then. You'll call me?"

"You're not seeing me at my best, I'm afraid."

Judith's eyes cleared for a moment and she remounted her bicycle.

"You are," she said, "the most devastating man I have ever met."

The bank wall flew off for a moment like a roller coaster of past ebullience, and when it returned to the walk Judith was gone. A sun shower commenced with a crack of lightning, and all at once the smell of wet asphalt catapulting through space reminded Mahoney of all the heartache of the first twenty-eight springs that had just up and gone.

Mahoney watched Nikki mosey past him in the twilight, reading what he assumed was a legal brief. She passed two people before walking face first into a parking meter. Mahoney had met her in court the day she had defended the mongoloid bitten by the police chief's dog; but she'd gone off to the Bahamas that same night and Mahoney could get no further than to offer to pick her up at the airport a week later.

Mahoney assisted her now to a bench and employed—there was nothing else—his athletic sock to absorb the blood. When she craned her neck backward in obedience to the wives' tale, Mahoney observed her neck and naturally glanced down her blouse.

"I hope you'll like them," Nikki said.

Mahoney wanted—he shook his head disapprovingly—to do drugs, codeine pills and Quaaludes, and to commit acts of little socially redeeming value with this woman.

"I apologize for leaving the airport after phoning." Nikki rested her hand on Mahoney's enclothed member. "The twins," she explained, "wanted to get back to Wayno in Manhattan, so I put them on the five-oh-five. I tried to phone again, but you were gone."

Mahoney had reservations about further involvement, since this woman was officially married with two little ones. Still, he seemed to be standing at attention and Nikki seemed prepared to pledge her allegiance.

"Do you give haircuts?" she asked, opening one eye.

Mahoney inferred this to be some cryptic come-on and admitted he never had but always wanted to.

"I have the necessary equipment," she said.

Once they'd returned to Mahoney's place, Nikki showered to soak her hair as Mahoney watched the moon focus in the gloaming. Then Nikki was on her knees in a chair before the bathroom's full-length mirror. Her black hair was wet and combed straight back. She'd taken one of Mahoney's T-shirts to conceal something of herself, but her most biblical of zones was godlessly naked. Of course, this temptation was supposed to be—and was!—insuperable, though Mahoney accepted her beneficence only after layering the last six inches of her hair. But for such a frenetic thing while on the go, Nikki went precipitately apoplectic on the kitchen table, and all the gyres of pleasure Mahoney envisioned remained a disincarnated figment of his imagination.

Nikki confessed she'd married the first man she'd "fucked" —Wayno—and hadn't "fucked" another in ten years, "until just now." Mahoney could tell, and felt like a slob for his disappointment.

With Nikki gone the owl hooted just to remind Mahoney of how much springtime could make the lonely hurt. He found himself drinking to fill in the little leaks of his drug narcosis. There was nothing but trouble ahead, and Mahoney wondered how undignified his gestures might become if he was forced to live a long life. He dialed Judith several times but hung up to the bark of John Hancock.

Some days, most days, life went as crass and desultory as an amusement park—one ride or game after another, and by the end you wanted to throw up. Mahoney had more tickets than he knew what to do with.

He listened to messages on the telephone answering machine while staring at an empty wine bottle. Nikki was phoning from the bus depot to apologize for leaving the airport without waiting. She confessed to missing him while in Bimini "with just Patty and Teddy and no man. I spent two solid days on the beach thinking about what a lovely item you must carry around with you and then I slept with a woman for the very first time."

Mrs. Elbush phoned from the mental health clinic to upbraid Mahoney for missing another session without prior cancellation. She proposed next week at the same time and place and recommended that Mahoney pay his overdue bill upon arrival.

Then one I. M. Packer rang from the credit bureau. "Your Stereo World account has been placed with us for immediate collection and calls for payment in full at once. Be helpful and we shall withhold further action for seven days." The same time, Mahoney remembered, it took God to make the world and rest up.

Finally Olive checked in from home with two 714s down the hatch. "Just wanted to know if you felt like comin' over with fraids for . . . wail, a groupie or somethin'." The sound of her voice was so sloppy it made Mahoney think of eating baked beans with a spatula.

Mahoney then remembered one more thing and stumbled into the night and round the house. The lilacs were showing incipient green buds in the floodlight and Mahoney wanted so much for this to move him.

Next to the office door, beneath the budding forsythia, Mahoney discovered a letter in his mailbox from—Christ!—I. M. Packer, announcing that "this account must have your prompt cooperation to avoid prosecution."

Meanwhile, the usual cartons and cages of the discarded were scattered beneath the mailbox: a litter of rabbits, seven unweaned kittens, two guinea pigs, and in a shoe box a hairless gerbil with a bacterial infection that kept it scratching its eyes. A note had been taped to the box of the unweaned kittens: TO WHOM IT MAY CONCERN—DISPOSE OF PROPERLY! Mahoney wondered how much longer he could keep his heart devoted to correcting so many little indecencies.

Judith rang. "Please don't dawdle."

Mahoney had his hands full with feeding bottles and antibiotic creams. It was nearly midnight and Judith was ready to move out.

Pharaoh Sanders intoned, "Love is everywhere," and Mahoney, staring into the night, wanted to believe it. The hairless gerbil was slippery as egg yoke from the ointment, but one little eye had opened and Mahoney kissed the damn thing.

"I implore you to hurry," Judith implored. "John Hancock is drunk and being restrained by the sheriff just outside this window."

Mahoney arrived just in time to see Chaney apply his billy club to John Hancock's right temple. J. H. had invited the clubbing by reaching for Chaney's .357 magnum; now he was in cuffs in the rear of the sheriff's Ford.

"Hidy, Popeye."

"Jesus died for nothing, Chaney."

Mahoney started for the stairs and John Hancock shouted, "No man ever crossed my prick-et line and lived long!"

At the stairs' summit, Judith hugged him with one arm while holding a birdcage in her slender hand.

"That bird looks sick, Judith."

"It is dead." She turned around to pick up a lamp.

"Forgive me for being in such a twit on the phone. That man has me freaking out."

Judith was barefoot in a black cotton skirt that was streaked with dryer lint. She wore a blue sweat shirt zipped up the center just above the swelling of those mysterious bosoms Mahoney couldn't ever seem to stop wanting.

"I'm so sorry you're always seeing me at my worst."

Mahoney would be twenty-nine and a quarter forty-three days before Judith turned thirty-eight, and when you had gone through the first thirty-seven with two ex-husbands, one a suicide and the other a shit, why then Mahoney felt he should be the one to apologize for being just another tramp come into her life.

"You ever wonder what happened to all of us?" Judith asked.

"I don't discuss those things with myself anymore."

Mahoney hoisted two suitcases. Judith was staring.

"I'm afraid I haven't any direction in my life without a man. I dislike myself immensely for telling you this."

Mahoney shrugged and carried the suitcases downstairs. "Direction" was a funny word and he disliked it; we were all directed toward the same thing. But strangely it made things matter more to Mahoney, not less. There was simply no meaning without deadlines.

Mahoney stepped into the night.

John Hancock shouted, "I'll kill the harlot!" and was driven away, in the direction of the county jail.

By the time Mahoney had carried the last box into Phyllis's place, Judith was asleep on the bare mattress in her skirt and sweat shirt and dirty bare feet. Her age was showing beneath her eyes and Mahoney cut the lights, covered her with an afghan, and lay down beside her. Moonlight formed bars on the wall beside them and Elaine wanted to know why Mahoney had asked her to leave after occupying the three best child-bearing years of her life. Mahoney's response was to drive away as quickly as possible.

The road was an aqueous blur, but the windshield wipers were irrelevant. Elaine said, Good, cry goddamn you! and Mahoney wondered if this act of penitent flight might mean she would leave him alone now.

Either way, he intended to call Mrs. Elbush in the morning about this ghost of his.

# THIRD DAY

DAY

Mahoney saw the sun rise above the eastern shore of the lake from his perch on a rock amid a turmoil of beached driftwood. An old pier extended a ways into the black lake before dissolving into wreckage and going under. The sun glowered there, suggesting Mahoney quit looking for excuses and signs of ubiquitous ravage. Still, passing through the trees, the wind whispered Harrisburg.

Mrs. Elbush, meanwhile, regretted that she could not see him until next week and advised him to perform one constructive act a day until then. We live by available light, Mahoney concluded, and there simply wasn't enough to go around. He wasn't one of the select, it seemed, but he assumed this implied that his depravity spared someone else the pain of the faithless life. His funk lifted with the lake fog once he determined his one good act would be to buy a drink for a thirsty bum at The Last Stop.

At lunchtime Mahoney spotted Judith lecturing before a small crowd on the library steps, and parked the van. So few aspired to saintliness in the days of God that Mahoney marveled at how some persisted even now that He was so obviously a bad anthropological joke.

Judith was standing to the right of a nuclear power plant diagram, but from Mahoney's perspective it seemed as though a cooling tower crowned her head. She flipped the sheet and the outline of a naked man—testicles and all—made the children scream.

"The thyroid gland is the most sensitive and most readily absorbs iodine 131." Judith drifted off a moment, glancing sadly into space. Directly she resumed her presentation, speaking with classroom precision. "The liver stores cobalt 60, the kidneys ruthenium 106; our bones and especially our children's bones absorb radium 226, zinc 65, strontium 90, promethium 147, barium 140, and thorium 234. The lungs collect radon 222, uranium 233, plutonium 239, and krypton 85."

Mahoney had heard enough, and ventured round the block. On his return, Judith took Mahoney by the hand to the van and asked him to take her away. They drove to the waterfall adjacent to the gun factory and watched the white water fall through space.

"I'm so naïve," Judith said. "I must be mentally retarded."

"Hey," Mahoney said strangely, "you got courage, toots. You got class all over you."

Judith looked at him skeptically, and for his part Mahoney wondered what evasion he was affecting this time.

Judith groaned, "Oh, fiddlesticks!" and set her chin in her hands. She seemed generally inconsolable.

Mahoney asked if there were something he could do.

"Stop lamenting this secret loss of yours."

"I'm trying to submerge my heartache for you."

"Let's face it, you cannot."

"There is always this." Mahoney opened the glove compartment.

"My first husband used to shoot the stuff with a hypo."

"I can lend you a straw."

Judith glanced at her little wrist watch. "I'd better get back to work."

Mahoney got the message.

"I'm sorry," Judith said.

Mahoney turned the key and put his foot down.

At The Cafe, Mahoney took Judith's hand as she started out the door. "You're very brave," he told her.

Judith squeezed his hand and stepped to the street. "John Hancock has been locked away in the jailhouse for resisting arrest," she said without the slightest recognition of the heartache Mahoney's eyes could not belie.

"I feel so intolerably alone without you, Judith." Mahoney thought she smiled sadly.

"If I didn't have to write a speech for tomorrow's rally," she explained, "I'd love to see you."

Mahoney said he understood and began to roll up the window; Judith held it down with her two hands.

"I'm tired of impetuously falling for every man I think is special, okay?"

Mahoney carried a sandwich and a quart of High Life dressed in a brown bag into the park across from The Cafe and put his brain to the sun. This mitigated the pain of that last swig passing his lips before his thirst was quenched. He was almost asleep when he heard his name announced, and momentarily, because of the bright sun and drowsiness, the world was black and white in his eyes. Nikki was waving from the road in a jogging suit.

"I want to talk with you," she called. "How's tonight?"

Mahoney's head nodded up and down and Nikki didn't lose a step, shouting, "My place at seven then."

Mahoney returned to the hot white light that provided surcease at no charge. He wondered about this ambitious woman who jogged on her lunch break but responded cadaverously to his sexual expertise. He could feel this woman's sublimation life style as a horse collar of absence about what in grade school he called his boner.

●    ●    ●

Before calling it quits, Mahoney corralled three runaway goats
feeding on the median of the interstate and arrested two unem-
ployable types setting muskrat traps in the stream bisecting the
city park. He found Judith at dusk between library stacks,
prostrate amid a chaos of papers and books pried open to vital
pages. She was wearing black leotard stockings beneath a green
skirt, which had collected high up her thighs; her baggy gray
sweater had holes in the elbows and hung in a loose scallop
around her throat and freckled chest. Mahoney called "Yo"
and lay down beside her on the papers, making a racket of
crinkling. Some peevish savant piped, "Really now!" Judith
was studying a chart of horizontal and vertical monopolization
within the energy field and seemed overwhelmed with indigna-
tion.

"I am so goddamned pissed off!" Her hand hooked a slant
of hair behind her flowered ear and she shook her head abjectly.
"I can't even begin to articulate this collusive intrigue to people;
they don't have the political smarts to deal with it." She let one
of her elbows collapse and rolled onto her back. Her eyes
closed. "The world is controlled by profiteers and pirates."

The savant in the carrel one stack back marched up with his
hands on his hips and glared at the two of them. Judith said,
"Transcend it, sourpuss!"

They went outside, where Judith paced back and forth while
Mahoney smoked a Chesterfield. When he tried to light a second one, Judith slapped it away and kept right on bouncing,
flicking manic little lefts and rights to Mahoney's deft counter
slaps, one of which caught her accidentally on the chin and left
her vanquished in Mahoney's apologetic arms. "If you hurt
me," she said softly, "it will be the very end of Ms. Chapters."

They both glanced up, found the flag flapping in a southern
breeze direct from Harrisburg, and Mahoney hoped those were
lightning bugs twinkling in the twilight. He felt all the burdens

of being seventeen again and holding a girl in his arms for the first time. It occurred to him in mid-embrace that one needed a specific type of love for someone in order to become even semi-human; and he feared if he didn't get on with it time might just run out on him.

"If my light is on later," Judith told him, "please come up."

Then she returned to the library.

NIGHT

At seven o'clock, fresh from a shower, as they say, Nikki was frenetically at work on dinner, scrabbling about the apartment without drawers in a snug black cotton top that ended in a V front and back; her dime-store flip-flops clapped salubriously enough to make Mahoney think of how coitus would surely tranquilize this longing for—what? Judith?

When Nikki located her designer jeans behind the sofa, she kneeled on the cushions and reached over shamelessly. This mooning left Mahoney nostalgic for Olive, and he reviewed all over again the role of licentiousness in this last year of the decade *Time* pronounced "exhausted." He determined compassion was our only move; and therein decided to give Nikki a second chance.

Observing her struggle to yank the zipper past the luxuriance of hair, Mahoney felt all the discipline of a wealthy depressive on a shopping binge. Nikki really did need assistance with that zipper, and Mahoney knew damn well it was not time to beat around the bush.

"How can I make it good for you?"

Moments later the jeans were on their own again and Nikki was comfy on the sofa, her legs an opened invitation. She employed the musical scale to indicate her degree of pleasure, and when it was just right Mahoney heard a consistent crooning of

Do Me, Do Me, Do Me. Afterward there was the requisite mashing of teeth and collision of tongues in order that Nikki might taste herself.

Obviously, Mahoney was never one to renounce drugs in the presence of radiant flesh that promised more to come. The 714 made him just wise enough with "a false sense of well-being," as *Time* admonished, that midway through the Billie Holiday album he discovered the quintessential nexus between Nikki's legal and sexual life: she had a profoundly exclusive predilection for the oral.

What they ate at the dinner table was spaghetti. Nikki was loose as one can be without falling into a sump narcosis. When she mentioned, lids at half-mast, that the caloric impact of two mouthfuls of a guy's "load" was roughly equivalent to half a box of linguini, Mahoney—idiotic on the Rorers—wondered if this meant that all fat people gave blow jobs. The conversation, in a word, took on all the vulgarity of a White House tape.

"How kinky can you get, Mahoney?" Nikki had her tits plunked down in the spaghetti but didn't seem to mind.

"Your left elbow is in my salad." Mahoney pointed and knocked over the wine. Nikki employed his underwear to tidy up.

"Would you mind?"

"Mind what?"

"Letting Nikki have . . . that item of yours one more time."

Mahoney craned his neck to observe her beneath the table but, straining a vertebra, settled for massaging her hair.

Afterward Nikki said, "Now kiss me."

Mahoney didn't exactly say no, but he took a swing at her.

"So!" Nikki said. "This means you've never slept with a man before."

"No'm," Mahoney said, not quite following this barbiturate logic.

"Never want to . . . Mooney?"

"No," Mahoney said.

"Never do two girlies at once?"

"No."

"Never want to?"

"Oh yes," Mahoney smiled.

"Mooney know any we might like?"

"What's your husband think of this?"

"Wayno's in Manhattan."

"Wayno's hip?"

"Hippo's gay."

"Your husband's gay?"

"Wayno's gone gay on us."

Nikki descended between his legs again; her eyelids were just having the damnedest time keeping open.

"You're drooling," Mahoney said, and he wondered what it would take to leave this woman happily sated.

"Usually do sucking *item*!"

"You all right there?"

"Wanna 'nother 'lude."

Nikki stood, though not without knocking her head twice on the table, and then mimed a spastic ballerina en route to her pocketbook.

"What's this?" She studied the yellow Ticonderoga with the hard pink tip at close range but seemed utterly baffled.

"You wanted a 'lude," Mahoney reminded her.

She looked at him.

"I am known to more than one litter . . . one little girl as Mommy."

This incoherence might have gone on and on had Nikki not passed out.

Judith's lights were extinguished, but there was a note for him on the door leading to the second floor.

I've found enough perfectly infuriating bits and pieces of hooliganism within the energy cartel to pester even the most virginal capitalist pirate. Meanwhile, the government's call for divestiture is more a complicitous charade than a serious dialectical challenge, since the darlings that traipse back and forth between government and industry in their FBI-gray suits seem to be the same cast of villains year after year.

But we shall defeat these twits yet,

Love, JC

P.S. I'm afraid I haven't been much fun of late. I did miss you tonight!

Elaine sat beside him on the ride to the bar and reminded Mahoney he was an eternal thorn in the heart of decency. He defended his right to philander freely amid so much disaster, then they both agreed his mind had a distinct penchant for the gutter. She seemed genuinely appalled at his dissolution into Rorer 714s and asked whatever happened to that plan of his to homestead and lead the good life. Mahoney confessed it had become just one more demerit in his accumulating ledger of desertions.

Olive was wearing her buckskin blouse and black leather pants. She took Mahoney's fiver and brought back change with a double Old Times and a chaser.

"I hear you been blowin' your wad all over town!"

"Ha, ha."

"Little Johnny Apple Seeder!"

The big-league boozers, stool for stool, were each in place. There was no need to emblazon their names on their jerseys; everyone knew them.

"Harold out cruising for burgers?"

Olive canted closer, pressing her twin swellings against the bar's gleaming.

"Harold's been doin' that airport rent-a-car chippy all week. And you best stow the whimsy, buster."

Mahoney knew they would all renounce him in the end: it was simply the logical dramatic evolution of his self-disgust. Maybe one of them would get mad enough and do him in before too long. Meantime, he polished off the Old Times, and the bell jar that kept him locked in—or out—evaporated in direct proportion to the death of those irreplaceable brain cells.

Olive was back with a shot on the house and an expression of conciliation. Mahoney knew this forecast a need to play normal, but there was no way he could get up for it.

"You wanna do me nice for a change?"

"Name it, baby."

Olive snorted. "Come on, buckeroo, I know you're just a nice boy."

Mahoney winked.

"You just head over with me to the diner after closin' 'cause ah'm not feelin' inclined to be by my lonesome."

"Yes'm."

"That's my lollipop."


The white tiles of the diner's interior sparkled as invitingly as a venerable public bathroom. Olive ordered pork chops and French fries with cranberry sauce; Mahoney remembered the first time he went to dinner with Elaine and thought he might weep till he died. Before it all went bad between them, eating with her in restaurants had been more fun than a barrel of monkeys.

He ordered a cup of tea with cream and tried to get a hold of himself. Olive wanted to know if Mahoney was "some Jew or somethin'."

"*What!*"

"Then how come you're drinking *cream* in tea?"

"Because I am a Jew, Olive."

"Ah just bet you are, nose job!" Olive allowed her skepticism to blow out her nose. "You're too damn dumb to be a Jew, boy!"

Olive's chops came and she smothered her fries in ketchup. Mahoney watched her eat. She held the pork bone close for inspection and then went right ahead on and sucked off the gristle.

"Ah can do more than just fuck, you know."

Mahoney said he hoped she was enjoying his company.

"What makes you think ah'm so stupid, snotrag, that you won't ever talk *seriously* with me?"

"I'm just a humane officer, Olive."

"Chaney says you went to the Ivy League and learned to write porno?"

"I majored in heartbreak, Olive."

Olive lowered the little pig bone and affected an air of dignity. "Ah am more than a collection of bodily holes, fucker face."

Mahoney felt defamed. "It's been a long one for all of us, Ollie."

"You could just try sharin' yourself!" The indignity registered belatedly and Olive heaved the bone at Mahoney when he least expected it. *"Don't you dare call me Ollie!"*

Mahoney would have been embarrassed, but the place was empty and the short-order cook was examining something he'd exhumed from his nose. Mahoney returned the bone to Olive's plate. She dipped a French fry into his tea and dropped it daintily into her mouth.

"Ah suppose you enjoy brangin' out the wurst in people?"

Mahoney apologized and asked if Olive had ever slept with a woman.

"Ah bet you'd love to hear all about it, sick boy."

He explained that a woman he knew had seen Olive at the bar and had fallen in love with her. "She wishes to sleep with us," Mahoney said.

"I cannot believe your mind."

"I just thought I'd let you know."

Olive pushed around her French fries with a fork and then meditatively mashed her cranberry sauce. "Looks like what them doctors make my kids into."

Mahoney just nodded. Then he looked into the street, to the sewer grate, for his moral compass.

"I suppose you think it would be fun?" Olive said.

"I suppose it might."

On their way out, Olive said, "Wail, maybe I will, and then maybe I won't."

The moon was full and Mahoney couldn't sleep. He walked to the degenerate pier with an Airedale who'd been carrying on dolefully in the garage. The terrier followed the aqueous path of moonlight on her swim until she disappeared in the darkness, and Mahoney was tempted to follow suit. He slipped into his own abyss and amid the detritus on the beach gazed up at the blue twinklers. He thought the same thing every drunken descendant of Cro-Magnon man ever thought while on a nighttime beach all alone. The terrible truth—and Mahoney acknowledged it—was that he didn't want to either sink or swim. The Airedale, meanwhile, emerged from the blackness with a giant bass in her mouth and soaked Mahoney shaking dry.

Mahoney made her lie beside him in the bedroom and fell asleep cradling what was left of his, well, *pathetic* share of the American Dream.

# FOURTH DAY

Chaney said, "You sleepin'!"

Mahoney's response was an admixture of curse and prayer of forgiveness. He wondered if the unseasonable heat wave might be the result of, say, a plutonium meltdown.

"Seems like the Woolworth's tryin' to sell them frickin' little turtles again," Chaney shouted. "Health people say they gots selminilla, so go pick 'em up. *You hear me?*"

"Uh-huh."

"You sick?"

"Misplaced my adjustment neurosis."

*"Act like a normal Christian soldier!"*

Jesus was not around to present Mahoney with a medal for brushing his teeth and dressing in a mere two hours' time while the hangover fairy rode a pogo stick between his ears. He took the Airedale along to remind himself that by a simple pat on the head he was capable of introducing a little happiness into the irradiated world.

Health Inspector Hackett and Mahoney quibbled over the confiscated turtles. Hackett insisted his department had exclusive disposal authority over all contaminated food and manufactured products. Mahoney reminded him that turtles were neither food nor manufactured products and kept the box of two hundred hatchlings stashed under his arm.

"Children eat those things!" Hackett was a regular bureaucratic maelstrom, complete with big ass and key rings on his belt loop. Mahoney didn't like his type and let him know it.

"The mayor shall hear about your mouth!" Hackett promised.

"Fuck the mayor!"

*"What did you say?"*

Mahoney said it more slowly, making one syllable two. Hackett demanded Mahoney's full name and badge number, holding paper and pencil at the ready. Mahoney hocked straight up and the wind took the snotwad to the north. He thought about those cows lined up at the fences and just couldn't generate a goddamn about this cretin standing before him in the parking lot.

Hackett employed a green hankie to mop his brow. *"Those goddamned things should be incinerated at once!"*

He lunged for the box; Mahoney pirouetted and drew his revolver.

"Why . . . why!" Hackett was paralyzed with astonishment.

Mahoney was in the cab with the Airedale, watching the high school girls blow lunchtime joints in the park, when Chaney called on the CB.

"Mayor wants them turtles and you in his office lickety-split!"

"Fuck him."

*"What!"*

Mahoney drove out to the lake and opened the box of turtles. They were red-eared sliders, the kind he raised in that distant epoch of his boyhood. He let them go in pairs into the cold water and they scurried straight down for safety. In the end, he could see scores of little green heads, at varying distances from shore, poking above the surface, musing at the sun.

• • •

The dachshund had fallen into the sewer and broken its leg. Mahoney climbed in head first for the rescue. Widow Fischman was so happy to have Adolph back that she treated Mahoney to chocolate-chip cookies and beer. The mayor signaled on the CB at three o'clock.

"What's this *we* hear about you spitting in Health Inspector Hackett's face?"

"Negative, Mayor."

"Now, did you or did you not draw a revolver on him? Yes or no."

"He kicked for my vitals."

"Say who?"

"Over and out, Mayor."

It all came crashing down in an urgency for Judith Chapters. Chaney signaled on the CB to say a blonde with a flower upside her ear had just paid one hundred dollars bond for the release of John Hancock, charged with resisting arrest.

Mahoney found Judith preparing tofu salad at The Cafe.

"Dry these, please." She nodded to a stack of dishes.

"What's this I hear about—"

"He's promised to go for treatment."

"Of what?"

"That horrible alcoholism."

"And you believe him?"

"He can be the most endearing man on earth."

"He's been a drunk for thirty years."

"You just can't abandon people on whimsy."

"He *attacked* you, Judith."

"*While* inebriated."

"When am I supposed to see you?" Mahoney hung up the towel of his participation.

"I fully intend to see you at the rally."

"I must insist on seeing you thereafter."

"Then so you shall."

"I'll keep my fingers crossed."

"You needn't bother with that."

Mahoney turned under the EXIT neon, wanting to speak; but he knew there was nothing to express but sadness and regret. He lowered his head and remembered the feeling of Elaine's shoulder below his forehead. He wondered what this sudden grief signified, and he concluded probably nothing much. Surely not a call to Elaine. Why there should be this one fatal roller skate on his stairway to easement with Judith—well, this too seemed beyond him.

"Tut tut, now," Judith said.

Apparently he had it written all over his face.

The commentator's makeup was not subtle, and his voice, piping from the TV's rear, reported radiation readings were three to four times higher in Mahoney's whereabouts than normal, though experts insisted this posed no *immediate* health hazard. Mahoney assented to this critique, acknowledging out loud that leukemia's latency period was anywhere from ten to thirty years. All at once, in one wink of the camera, the nation's ruling-class spokesman, known to the sycophantic as Mr. President, filled the screen. Mahoney saw a shocking resemblance to Howdy Doody.

*"I have great confidence in American technology, American innovation, American courage, and the will of the American people . . ."*

Another wink of the camera and the commentator said:

*"Officials at Metropolitan Edison Company, the utility operating the plant at Three Mile Island, acknowledged for the first time two unprecedented and inexplicable explosions of hydrogen gas in the reactor core."*

Mahoney switched stations in time to hear America's favorite anchorman gravely announce that *"a new congressional study reports the administration 'deliberately and grossly' exaggerated the effects of the Iranian oil cutoffs on the United States and that oil imports actually increased during the cutoff rather than dropped by half a million barrels a day."*

An ensuing commercial message by America's bankers promised they were "changing things for the better"; Mahoney glanced out the window. The whitecaps on the lake were rolling to the north. Howdy Doody was back proclaiming that *"the primary and overriding consideration of all of us is the health and safety of the people of the entire area."* Mahoney assumed that he was somehow included and couldn't take it any longer. The Commander-in-Chief extinguished in a *plink* of imploding darkness that left only a little blue star in center screen.

Nikki thundered up the road in a battered Vista Cruiser redolent of her furtive suburban past. There weren't any children screaming in the station wagon rear, but it sure as hell was easy enough to imagine.

Mahoney was hosing the doggy run and felt no contrition giving Nikki a squirt to the abdomen. She cried out, but the black wet suit's protection left them each smiling foolishly in the fallout. Mahoney helped her lug the yellow air tanks to the lake and then her athletic bod, flippered and masked, plunged into the lake and went under just where the rotting pier did the same. The Airedale turned back, bewildered. Mahoney stood at shore smoking and feeling all the portentous dread the astrologer said water should evoke in him. He imagined water filling his lungs and jogged indoors to strap himself into his rocking chair for the impending anxiety attack.

Nikki surfaced at his covetous worst: two minutes before dinner. He surprised himself by begrudging her half *his* baked potato and salad. He wanted silence, but Nikki had the attorney's urge to blather and so detailed the disquieting anatomical consequences of her jailbird client's favorite pastime: Greek gang-banging. She admitted that her husband engorged a finger or two in her "asshole" in those early days of their infrequent mating, but she found the procedure too reminiscent of her gynecologist's biannual polyp hunt to get excited by it. But *he did*, so who could explain men's fascination with the ass? She asked Mahoney what he thought of all this, and he mentioned, for the fourth time, that he really was trying to eat his dinner, which had no impact on this peripatetic woman, who resumed the conversation by asking what the big to-do was with reaming.

Mahoney requested she put a temporary cork in her flow of depravity.

"Why can't people *speak* about what they do?" she wanted to know. "I think sexual feedback is *important.*"

"Pass the salt."

"Why are you being so defensive?"

*"Because I am trying to eat my supper!"*

"I have a husband three hours away from here who will sit across from me eating his supper and ignore me."

Mahoney gazed up from his potato skin and opened his mouth wide. Salad tumbled out as he made a puking sound. "How's that? Nice?"

Nikki was undaunted.

"What about this woman? Have you arranged something?"

"Tentatively."

"Well, I can't do it this weekend because Wayno and the kids will be visiting."

"Perhaps they might watch."

"I rather doubt that."

"Tea?"

"What?"

"Tea!"

"No!"

She stood up, removed her wet suit, top and bottom, and walked to the bathroom. Inevitably her showering evoked memories of Elaine, and Mahoney remembered things that can only hurt you. He wondered why his dick should be at once contiguous and incompatible with his more abiding moral sensibility. *The act,* he realized, was just another contemporary leisure sport, and the porno stores were keeping pace by stocking as many new and nifty aids as the running stores displayed imported shoes and suits. Mahoney feared he might be wising up.

He left Nikki a note saying he'd be in touch and absconded to the van. A robin was trilling softly and Mahoney, disbelieving, said a prayer for the world. Then he was on his way to a rally of citizens who were dedicated to something more than their own worst instincts.


NIGHT

The earnest congregated in the small park across from the library. Mahoney leaned against a maple tree whose limbs were heavy with little red blossoms. The moon was luminescent in the seven o'clock twilight, and Mahoney was looking straight up, as an Airedale does espying a squirrel in an overhanging limb, when Judith Chapters approached him. She blew his mind by reaching for a cigarette and lighting up. Mahoney just couldn't help himself over this woman.

"What's this?"

"The weed?"

"Yes."

"I'm scared to death."

She visibly trembled at the sight of the animated rabble on the lawn before the podium. Someone with a feather in his hat and three earrings was distributing white candles, which people were busily lighting. Mahoney remembered the little lightning bugs of his youth, whose abundance was, so to speak, controlled by the family lawn and garden centers which promulgated enough Union Carbide, Dow, Chevron, and Ortho sprays, dusts, de-weeders, and feeders to send this flickering little species to that more rarefied state called physical extinction.

"People like myself," Mahoney said, wanting to embolden, "depend on people like yourself."

Judith blew smoke from her nose, choking slightly.

"The weak," Mahoney asseverated, "are in search of the strong."

Someone chanted, *"No nuke puke! No nuke puke!"* and the congregation joined in, clapping in concert.

"I cannot do it!" Judith moaned.

"Extinguish that butt and get your shit together."

She looked at the weed and moaned, "You're right," but took one more drag. Someone on the podium was playing the *only* golden oldie from the Phil Ochs *oeuvre,* and someone else, to the left of the guitarist, waved a white handkerchief at Judith. "If I can't get people to self-activate over this issue," she said, "I'll self-destruct instead." She glanced at her note cards and sighed. "Say something to make me strong."

"Eighty years from now this won't make a dent or a difference."

*"Yes it will, schmucko! Look at the babies here!"*

Mahoney thought of the three hundred nuclear plants scheduled for construction by the turn of this most gruesome of centuries and tried to remember one of those prayers his first-grade teacher led with bowed head at quarter to eight, five days a week, until the court told her to cool it.

Judith said, "Hold my hand while I'm up there—promise?" and disappeared into the crowd before Mahoney could cross his heart and hope to die.

John Hancock tapped Mahoney's shoulder and Mahoney

had to look for that treed squirrel to meet him eye to eye.

"Keep your skewer outta my babe, brother!"

He was ominously close, with his hands on Mahoney's throat, so Mahoney just had to put the loaded revolver—which he was authorized to carry in order to halt, say, a dog's pursuit of a deer—to this devil's chin.

"I'm counting to three. One . . . two . . ." Hancock fled, toting a jug of wine.

Mahoney spotted Olive standing with Harold by the town's honorary war monuments. The dead were listed in alphabetical order. Olive was holding the sodas and Harold the French fries. They each had their own little patty of charcoal-broiled steer flesh on a white flour roll, and it sure did smell good. Olive turned at Mahoney's whistle and, when she spotted him beneath the tree, gave him the finger. Elaine was seated beside Mahoney, whispering yet another scurrilous denunciation, but this had the advantage of inuring him to abuse by the time Olive arrived.

"Ah s'pose the next thing you'll want is to put a collar and leash on me."

"I didn't know you were one of the disaffected, Olive." Mahoney was impressed with this display of concern.

"I most certainly ain't! Whatsoever that means."

Judith stepped to the microphone and people applauded.

"Harold wants to know can he join us," Olive said, chewing.

"Tell him to come over."

"Not *us*, *here*, brain-damaged. Your lady friend and you and me."

"*You told him!*"

"Why not? He makes me sleep with his colored friends."

"Is there no limit to our perfidy, Olive?"

"You heard me clear, prince."

"Tell him game's closed."

"Then maybe I just won't do it myself."

Mahoney shrugged, then shifted in time to catch her knee in his hip.

"Tomorrow night or nothin'," she said.

"Impossible. The woman has visitors."

"What kind of visitors?"

"Husband and progeny."

"Two of my little *its,*" Olive reflected, "got flushed down the bowl. Third it I gave to an Indian woman for a week's worth of needle."

"Age makes us sentimental."

Olive bristled. "You may think you're funny, sonny, but you're just another sexy creep ah merry fuck."

"This discourse is beginning to attract flies."

"Ah'll be at the bar tomorrow from noon on through, so you know where to find me."

She pushed her hip into Mahoney and departed. Judith was rolling:

"Finally, the UPI quoted Governor Thornburgh as saying that he believed"—she glanced at her cards—"that the hundreds of thousands of people who live near the reactor in Harrisburg *can be persuaded* that the danger is being brought under control." Judith's eyes twinkled at Mahoney and then she looked beyond him. "But already one hundred thousand citizens have fled on their own! Because *they* shall not *persuade* us to accept this charade of safety. We must work toward a general strike to cripple nuclear proliferation!"

There was polite applause from the audience of candle bearers and Judith shook the hand of the guitar player, who started strumming again. John Hancock rushed onto the podium and embraced Judith, who threw a left hook to his ear to express her disapprobation. Hancock went to his knees, spilling red wine, and Judith plunged into the crowd.

• • •

They drove in the van up the mountain and, lying on a blanket on the roof, watched the stars. It was a black open sky and the density of the stars formed a mist of bluish light. Miles below, they could see the town's constellation of lights.

"The point is," Judith whispered, "that the same profiteering system that dropped nearly twice as many bombs on Cambodia in '73 than on all of Germany in World War Two, and that defoliated Vietnam with deadly dioxin, is now *consciously* experimenting with the lives of this nation. We're all the guinea pigs of a handful of racketeering technocrats who want to automate industry more than protect our nation's populace."

Judith was well into her crusade. Mahoney kept cool. The stars, a million years from his small life, put things on Earth in, well, perspective.

"Judith?"

"Do you realize when they close down the nuke plants because of safety violations or technical screw-ups, our utility bill reflects the capital investment cost of that plant *plus* whatever alternative source of fuel they substitute, like coal or gas?"

From Mahoney's particular angle, looking up at her, Judith's head appeared in the stars.

"Judith?"

"I mean, Jesus Christ! There are reactors in Florida, South Carolina, Ohio, Arkansas, and California with the same design flaws and the goddamn Nuclear Regulatory Commission said no restrictions would be placed on them!"

"Judith?"

"The thing I *cannot* believe is that Metropolitan Edison tried to lease part of their poisoned island to farmers as grazing land for dairy cows. You know what they discovered last year bubbling in the ponds on the island? Xenon gas! Little kids are supposed to drink the milk from those grazing cows! And don't tell me the fuckers at Metropolitan didn't know all about the radioactive crud, because they were leasing the land at bargain prices—ten dollars an acre!"

"They've all gone home, Judith."

"One of these days, Mahoney, I'm going to finally meet a man that I love well enough to make a baby, and then the world will deform it before it has a chance. You know what low levels of background radiation do to a fetus?"

Mahoney's heart went out to this woman. But there seemed to be no lasting relief for any of us without pharmaceuticals, and Mahoney couldn't help but wonder if he would always be stupefied with sorrow and, in general, at a loss whenever he was sober.

When he got into bed that night, he phoned her. "Judith, I am scared sick without you."

He had her blue pail of lake odds and ends on the night table beside the bed, and he was collating, by candlelight, the imprints of one snail shell with the etchings on a stick. He kept placing them together to make a match.

"Dearest," Judith said, "I cannot talk to you now."

"No?"

"He is here. I'm so sorry. Good night."

At least the Airedale's head was on the pillow beside him, and they both lay on their backs, staring helplessly at the ceiling. He said, "Good night, Bosco," and fell asleep holding her available paw.

## FIFTH DAY

DAY

The morning was merciful with sun and Mahoney carried a
folding chair and a cup of coffee across the meadow and sat
before the lake. He removed his shirt and listened to the gulls
screaming on the rocks surrounding the red channel lighthouse.
Judith was everywhere in his mind. A formation of geese
honked in transit above the lake for the first time in a week and
the copse of poplars in the swamp near the road was yellow with
new leaves. But Mahoney didn't go for this renascence anymore, at least not like he used to. He wasn't interested in
investing his heart in a losing, if not lost, cause. But then he saw
the geese circle around from the north and descend through the
sun onto the lake. They came down in an explosion of calling.
Sunlight glittered on their wakes and eddies, and the gulls went
silent. Mahoney was helpless and saw it all again for the very
first time. The heartache left him in a panic, and when he
returned from the house he was armed with a pack of Chesterfields and a quart Tropicana bottle filled with iced screwdrivers.

When Judith dropped by at noon, Mahoney had to squint to
locate the lake. Judith said his little dinghy was lovely, so he
unfurled the mainsail from the boom and they tacked SSE at
close haul.

Judith hung her head to the lee and ran her hand in and out
of the lake.

"The horrible man shattered Phyllis's colonial glass door with a rock and just dumped his presumptuous self on my bed." Mahoney had been waiting patiently. "He was so abjectly smashed when I found him I phoned police headquarters to have someone remove him. Apparently he responded peculiarly this morning by butting his head on the bars. Then, when he learned that Phyllis had charged him with breaking and entering, he urinated on his cot, which seems to have been regrettable, as now they've sent him to Willard for psychological tests."

Mahoney prepared to change the tack. He saw the ripples dancing off the bow ten yards ahead and told Judith to duck-ho. He threw the tiller to starboard and the boom came racing across the little dinghy and kept right on going. It sounded like lightning striking and then Judith and he were staring at each other beneath the mainsail.

"Should I be concerned?" she asked.

Her blue pail of archeological treasures had spilled in the mayhem, and old buttons, bits of crockery, and porcelain were all about them.

Mahoney was stunned. The mast had snapped.

He pushed the nylon sail away and glimpsed the mast drifting east with the main line descending into the depths. Gulls were circling above in a halo of curiosity, and Mahoney figured they were watching termites drowning by the hundreds; the inside of the mast was hollow, and the rotten crumbs in his hand cleaved like grade-A sawdust should when put in contact with water.

He unclipped the sail from the mast and furled it the best he could. The termites' drowning rekindled all his own worst fears of going under himself, and he remembered the astrologer's admonition that he keep to solid ground. He used the rudder as a paddle and in the hour of rowing to shore, he and Judith agreed that monogamy was preferable to polygamy or the polymorphous perverse, since it isolated betrayal and abandonment to one at a time.

On the horizon, the vague mass of the moon could be discerned climbing in the afternoon sky. Judith was red from overexposure and leapt to shore with an ebullience he'd never before seen in her.

"What a fabulous little adventure this has been!" she said happily, but her eyes couldn't belie the thirty-seven years she'd survived; and this only served to heighten the pathos of this lady's fleeting happiness. Mahoney bent over to haul up the dinghy and Judith stowed her hand beneath his shorts.

"Oh good," she whispered. "I was hopeful I'd like your ass."

Mahoney supplicated Jesus for a home run, and he and Judith Chapters drifted into the tall grass near the alder trees. They were intent upon taking their chances.


NIGHT

Mahoney drove Judith to The Cafe at five. The wind abated with the dusk, and in the stillness the robin's threnody communicated all the gloominess of post-coitus *triste*. Judith wore white with hepatica flowers behind her ears. Mahoney was, he shuddered, in love with her.

Phyllis was setting silverware on the outdoor wooden tables and Judith made a crack about irradiating the outdoor customers. Phyllis quipped, "Harrisburg's your fetish, not mine!" "Harrisburg" was already beginning to sound Japanese to Mahoney, like Hiroshima, for example; but you'd find more than a few apologists for that transgression too.

Mahoney wanted nothing more from life than to wait in the van for Judith to come home with him. He got comfy and turned on CBS for the latest version of things. He could smell cream of broccoli steaming from Judith's subterranean kitchen and wondered, if he tried desperately enough, whether he might just succeed with this woman. He could swear he heard fallout sighing in the wind, but it turned out to be the flare of the sulfur match at his cigarette point, beyond which Mahoney spotted Nikki and three others approaching the restaurant. He released lung smoke through the window and Nikki walked into it.

"Twins!" she said, "say hello to Mahoney."

In unison, they failed to respond.

Nikki and the one the anemic little progenies most resembled wore red jogging suits.

"Wayno, this is Mahoney."

The grip of Mahoney's handshake diminished perceptibly when Nikki said, "Mahoney and I are lovers," but Wayno squeezed all the harder and said, "Beautiful! Shall we eat outdoors, girls?"

Wayno invited Mahoney to join them, but he declined. Wayno then submitted to the twins' tugging and drifted away to the tables.

"I can't believe you flushed!" Nikki leaned her elbows against the open window frame and centered her face in her hands. "I've already told you that Wayno and I are free to fuck whomever."

Douglas Edwards signed off and Judith appeared on the patio with a stack of plates and a red apron tied in place.

"Are you listening?" Nikki said.

Judith cocked an eye in a parody of suspicion and returned inside. Mahoney told Nikki that their friend Olive insisted upon getting together that night. Mahoney resolved it would be his farewell to profligacy, and for the first time in years he knew he meant it.

"Why tonight?"

"Whimsy."

"Why are you being sardonic?"

"Whimsy."

"Oh shit."

"I'll tell her it's off."

"Don't you dare!"

She turned and signaled with one finger for Wayno to come hither. He jogged over and Nikki explained that Mahoney had arranged a *ménage à trois* with a woman who was leaving town in the morning and would he mind if she left him at home with the twins tonight?

"Groovy!" Wayno said. "*Fantasia*'s playing on Home Box!"

Nikki kissed her husband's ear and said, "Look at Mahoney, dear; he's embarrassed for us."

Mahoney declined dinner a second time and arranged to meet Nikki at The Last Stop at nine. Nikki handed him eight 'ludes to distribute between Olive and himself, and then the police CB crackled with the news that a tall Caucasian male, six-five, in his mid-fifties, answering to the name of John Hancock, had escaped from the Willard Mental Asylum during recreation hour.

Mahoney found Judith's hand in the soup pot.

"Lost my ring!"

"John Hancock has escaped!"

"Oh dear!"

Judith requested overnight asylum at Mahoney's pad. He apologized for a previous engagement that would never ever happen again for the rest of their lives and handed her the keys to his house. He was preparing to put childish things behind him.

"Will I be alone all night?"

"There will be Bosco."

"Chocolate drink makes me ill."

Mahoney remembered that place beneath her hair behind her ear and told her that he loved her and wasn't scared about it, either.

Judith was thirty-seven and couldn't quite go for it.

"You are lovable," she said, "and unsuitable. The fatal combination."

"Sweet dreams, Judith."

Judith winked. *"Ciao,* kiddo."

Mahoney called Chaney and instructed him to keep an eye on the place.

Olive had them three deep at the bar with her translucent plastic pants and black panty hose. On her break she joined Mahoney at the door.

"Is she comin'?"

"I reckon so, Olive."

" 'Cause ah sat in a bath of oil beads the whole day through!" She rubbed her cheek against Mahoney's and his hands dropped reflexively for her seat.

"You best take us someplace swanky first off," Olive said, " 'cause ah'm absolutely starvin' to daith!"

"Now, listen, Olive . . ."

"Just don't get bossy, Spartacus!"

"We are all coequals in this."

"Treat me like a lady, boy!"

Mahoney withdrew a 714 the size of a Maalox pill and Olive swallowed it without water for speedy relief.

"You best keep 'er up for us tonight, hair pie, 'cause I want to see . . ." The 'lude lodged halfway down and Olive coughed it up and tried again.

" 'The rockets' red glare, the bombs bursting in air'?" Mahoney offered.

"You just do *your* thing and *we'll* do ours."

This resurrected memories of the Kangaroo Brothers versus the Golden Boy at the old Madison Square Garden wrestling ring, and Mahoney began to wonder where Olive's sexist head might be at. He speculated that this trinity of theirs would function best if cognitive acuity was tranquilized to the fullest illegal degree, and handed Olive a second 'lude.

Olive tossed the pill in the air like a jelly bean and took it in the mouth on the second step backward.

"Ah gotta get back now, you."

"Don't get sloppy back there, Olive."

Wayno and the twins dropped Nikki off in the Vista Cruiser. Nikki said Wayno said to ask Mahoney if he knew where the boys cruised after hours, and Mahoney told Nikki to tell Wayno to try the Cock-a-Doodle-Doo. Wayno beeped pulling out and he and the twins waved like circus freaks through the open windows. Nikki wore paisley-cloth high heels, tight red sweat pants, and a black halter top. Her black hair was pulled back tight in a ponytail.

"Neo-punk," she said.

"Olive's *odd* tonight."

"A threesome always is."

They stepped inside in time to see Jack Daniels slip through Olive's hands to the floor. This generated applause from the most-likely-to-be-cirrhosis cases, and all Olive could do was laugh and stumble off for the mop. The 714s had landed.

"Sexy," Nikki said. "You think she'll like me?"

Mahoney handed her his tomato juice and a Rorer with a wink. He knew that given the false merriment of the 'lude high, chances were better than even that, for better or worse, they would each enjoy their screwing.

"I do love her pants," Nikki said.

A man in a cowboy hat and gas station overalls leaned back in his chair and kept right on going in an accelerating arc to the floor.

"I feel slightly nervous," Nikki said.

"That mule pill should kick any minute now."

"We do make a lovely triangle."

Nikki glanced from Olive and withdrew folded sheets of

paper from her handbag. She and Mahoney took seats.

"You might want to peruse these," she recommended.

Mahoney opened the sheets to primitive sketches of three figures engaged in exotic geometries of congress.

"You draw these?"

"Wayno."

"What is this here?" Mahoney pointed to figure 1.

"Your instrument."

"I thought perhaps a Louisville slugger."

"Wayno's mordancy."

"And this?"

"Two women atop you, one straddling your slugger! And the other upon your kisser . . ."

"And this here?" Mahoney was hanging in there.

Nikki squinted. "A tongue?"

"Undoubtedly ingested by someone's . . . ?"

Nikki turned the picture to the side, then upside down.

"Ah! Olive squatting with you mounted from posterior while she stimulates me orally."

Mahoney moved on to diagram 3 and wondered, well, just *wondered* about himself. "This one I don't understand."

"That's Olive standing."

"And this?"

"You kneeling on a kitchen table, or any convenient elevated surface."

"With Olive absorbing . . ."

"Correct."

"With you working from the blind side. But what's this?"

"An aid."

"Something one straps on like the old cowpokes?"

"I told you I wanted to *fuck* a woman."

"And what if God is not really dead?" Mahoney inquired, slightly appalled.

Nikki touched his cheek. "Come of age, darling!"

• • •

At nine o'clock Olive floated over on her cloud of pharmaceutical bliss. Nikki stood up and introduced herself and Olive hugged her with one arm while reaching for Mahoney with the other.

"Ah want a motel room where the TV is colored."

"Marvelous!" Nikki had her arm around Olive's waist.

" 'K, fuckface?"

Mahoney nodded and glanced at figure 2 to get himself over the rough part.

"You're rather devastating in those pants," Nikki said.

"Ah'm a seamstress and compose poems, too. Not that buckeroo cares."

"Well," Nikki said, "I certainly do care."

Mahoney followed them to his doggy van, glanced at the bank clock, and swallowed one and a half 'ludes.

At the Hideaway, he and Nikki stepped into the office to sign the register. A voice issued from behind the screen door, and there stood Olive, swaying visibly in the windless night.

"Ah don't find this place acceptable. There ain't dining facilities."

Nikki was eager to accommodate Olive and conferred with her in whispers. Mahoney popped another half down the drain so his body would put any calls from his conscience on hold until sometime after daybreak. Olive, meanwhile, was mollified by a quick stop at the place that boasts how many charcoaled quarter-pound wounds of cattle flesh it has sold since the erection of those two plastic golden parabolas.

By midnight they were established on the third floor of the Nation's Innkeeper with two bottles of soave. Alcohol and 'ludes went together like a lighted match and leaking propane, and according to *Time* could be "dangerous in combination." But Mahoney was in a funk about death's revolving door and drank without leaving any for the fish. Besides, one look at Olive and Nikki and he knew he was a sucker for dangerous combinations.

When he returned from the shower, Nikki and Olive were lounging on the bed on their stomachs, studying Nikki's diagrams. Half a bottle of soave was gone and Nikki's aid was lying beside her. Mahoney discovered that another half was all he needed and drifted toward them through the bathroom's diffusing steam. He sat down beside them in a Holiday towel.

"Why don't I take off Olive's pants?" Nikki said.

"Whyn't you two just watch me take 'em down?"

Nikki and Mahoney remained on the bed as if watching the Saturday night movie until Olive, down to her black leotards, said, "I need a volunteer."

Nikki said, "I'll shoot you out, babes," and they recited, "Once, twice, three, *shoot!*" Mahoney lost.

Nikki knelt before Olive and had the leotards as far down as Olive's knees before she got distracted and found true love at nose tip. Mahoney couldn't remember if this was diagram 1, 2, or 3. Once he joined them, however, it all broke down into a game of grab and keep.

Mahoney knew he'd had enough when his back gave out near dawn and his two hernia scars needed oiling. Olive was kneeling at bed's end sucking his big toe when Nikki finally strapped her aid in place. Mahoney drifted away, musing at how tenuous those two and one-half little pills rendered civilization's hold on his improvident longings.

## SIXTH DAY

**DAY**

At noon Nikki and Olive showered together, locking Mahoney out. Mahoney had no choice but to employ an empty wine bottle for a urine sample as he watched a TV newscaster standing before three nuclear cooling towers. Nikki had to hurry home for brunch with the twins and Wayno, and Harold had undoubtedly been kept waiting for Olive to attend his father's ten o'clock sermon with him. Mahoney thought perhaps it would not be all bad if that plant blew sky high and settled selectively upon the depraved.

Judith was doing pranayamas on the beach. Mahoney raced past her into the lake, knowing full well that his soul required baptism if not drowning before it could ever qualify as cleansed.

"What have you been doing all this time?" Judith asked.

"Exorcising an habitual disposition."

"Oh dear."

When he stepped from the lake, Judith tossed him his jeans. He stood there drying off and picking duckweed from his shoulders. Judith studied his wand—sometimes less than magical, according to some—as Mahoney stepped bare-assed into his jeans. Meantime, Elaine fell from the sky and stuck a pin in his heart. Mahoney realized what it was about himself that he so much disliked: he was scared to death of all that hurt coming back and, simultaneously, sick and tired of holding hands with his own evasions.

"I'm not going to hate myself for not loving you," he told Elaine, and Judith said sullenly, "Forget it then!" She knelt down for a piece of amber glass and Mahoney fell to his knees beside her, confessed to being haunted by ghosts and feeling generally helpless, helpless, helpless. Still, he promised to shape up and act at least twice as old as his shirt's neck size.

"I'm willing to live," Judith said, *"as if* everything bad is behind us."

Mahoney turned around in time to catch his shadow fucking off again, and didn't know what to think.

In the woods surrounding the lake, Judith proved herself all erudition amid so much greenery. She knew flora as Mahoney knew varieties of party drugs. It seemed an important variance and Mahoney felt all the worse by comparison. When they reached the stream, Judith pointed and said, "Do you remember this?"

Mahoney squinted and tried to remember.

"Buttercup?"

"No, sweetheart. Coltsfoot."

The sun, meanwhile, beamed through the hemlocks in long golden shafts, and staring up, Mahoney wanted to rise from the floor like so many spiraling gnats, who were surely no better than he. Judith was fussing about, unearthing little delicacies —"Now, these marvelous little white flowers are bloodworts. And there," she was pointing, "over there is trillium. Aren't they lovely?"—when Mahoney stumbled to the ground to the snap of fracturing bones. It turned out to be a skeleton of some sort. Indeed, Mahoney had seen those hollow sockets before while shaving, and the specific angle of the skull, with the nasal passages kissing mud, seemed the perfect answer to that bit of curiosity Mahoney's father could never tire of positing: "Son,

I just can't hardly wait to see what you're like when you're finally all grown up!" Mahoney picked himself up from the bones, holding a hoof. "Coltsfoot?" His drollery, however, vanished when the yellowjacket stuck it to his cheek.

Judith pulled his hand away and examined his tear-stained cheek. Mahoney remembered Elaine saying, "Like all men, you're just a big baby!" and hid his face in Judith's bony shoulder.

His right eye swelled shut, and on their way back, when he attempted to look to the right, to Judith, without twisting his neck, all he saw was the slope of his nose, which he thought pretty well summarized the precise downward course of his ways.

"You look perfectly miserable," Judith said.

Mahoney went directly home to administer ice cubes wrapped in a baggy to his diminishing vision.


NIGHT

When he woke, his favorite commentator addressed the nation on the TV. Judith was seated beside him, holding ice to his cheek.

*"President Carter toured the Three Mile Island nuclear plant today as the problem of bleeding the hydrogen gas bubble from the reactor core remained unsolved. Government officials warned that a precautionary evacuation of thousands of people might be necessary.*

*"Meanwhile, the President and his wife spent thirty-five minutes reviewing the concrete outer shell of the crippled reactor from a yellow school bus that drove them between the cooling towers to the control room of the enormous plant."*

The President's raiment, Mahoney observed foggily, included a gray suit and blue tie with little yellow moon-man booties.

Judith said, "I hope the dreadful man is wearing a lead supporter."

Mahoney gazed out the window to the dusk with his one good eye. The moon cast shadows across the lake and might have been responsible for the poplar tops' phosphorescent glow, though Mahoney was beginning to think that his so-called ir-radiation paranoia had been fully validated by the facts. He closed the window with provident skepticism and pulled the blinds. Like Mahoney himself, radiation was just one more deadly product of the age.

The First Family stood in somber meditation before their constituents, the First Lady cradling an infant in her arms.

"For this media hype that handsome little boy will be dead of leukemia in fifteen years," Judith said.

"Judith?" Mahoney knew there was nothing left for him to do but start all over again, and he thought perhaps a resolution in concert with this woman might be appropriate.

"I am harboring treasonous thoughts about our nation's leadership," Judith said.

"Judith?" How a man of Mahoney's hopelessness could still maintain such bashfulness was certainly a mystery to him. He had the terrible feeling that perhaps he didn't know a damn thing about himself, except this: he was feeling cold and lonely and weary of it all. And it was getting old, getting him nowhere.

"Let's take a peek at that eye."

"Will you stay for dinner, Judith?"

"Would you like me to?"

"The world is failing all around us."

"Mahoney?"

"Yes, Judith?" Mahoney was prepared to answer, "And I love you too," when Judith Chapters said, "I am very, very hungry."

•　　•　　•

Mahoney found the last two quarts of homemade tomato sauce in the bottom rack of the freezer in the basement. On the freezer tape across the top was Elaine's handwriting, and Mahoney stared at "Tomato Sauce, August 15, 1978" until the feeling passed and let him breathe again. The dogs bayed dolefully from their menagerie, so he freed them to the full blessings of the poisoned run. He hadn't seen Bosco since the day before, and he found himself gloomy at the prospect that she'd run away. Still, this was a sure sign that his heart existed to do more than simply pump blood.

In the kitchen, Judith was squirting lemon juice over slices of cucumber.

"I positively dread being boring to another human being," she said. "The minute I bore you I'm leaving. I swear."

The frozen blocks of sauce in the blue enamel pot were smoking like those Harrisburg cooling towers on the TV, and Mahoney looked at her through the mist.

"After two months I just never have anything interesting to communicate," Judith said sullenly, and bit into the lemon. "I've never mentioned this to a soul before"—she winced— "but my second husband was so bored with me that he blew his brains out while taking me from behind one morning. Of course, John Hancock finds me engaging, but he's a drunkard."

Mahoney heard a deep sigh and thought, at first, it was his own reflexive commiseration. But Judith heard it too and, like Mahoney, frowned; then the Airedale, Bosco, emerged from under the tablecloth. Her nose lifted toward the spaghetti sauce and she stretched forward on her two front legs and lay down again, moaning. Mahoney wanted to frame this little moment of Norman Rockwell joy and hang it on his bathroom mirror so he'd never have to see himself again.

"Who's this?"

"Miss Bosco," Mahoney said.

"How pretty you are, Miss Bosco!"

Judith knelt down, and her long legs seemed the only redress Mahoney needed to keep afloat in the sinking world.

"If that plant melts down we've had it, kid." Judith addressed the Airedale from the spaghetti pot, where she was breaking a handful of semolina sticks in half. The pot of water began to roll with an ascension of bubbles and Judith dumped spaghetti into the pot.

"The frightful thing about radiation," she muttered, watching the water, "is how it forces you to cram a normal life of silly little pipe dreams into a latency period of fifteen to thirty years." She stirred the spaghetti in the water and Mahoney noticed a bleariness in her eyes. "Isn't it funny," she said, "how the facts tend to tear the heart right out of us."

Mahoney went to Judith Chapters and stood beside her, leaning hip to hip, and watched the spaghetti churn in the oily water. Judith just said the kind of things he had always wanted them to say—brave and intelligent and sorrowful things. Mahoney embraced her timidly with the kind of emotional intensity that comes along every three hundred pairs of arms or so. He told her something intimate, employing a four-letter word.

"I'm so glad."

"I am sick of irony."

"I suppose it must be hideous being you."

"And now I love you," Mahoney said again.

Judith took his hand and stared. "All I have ever wanted," she said quietly, "throughout my entire life is a decent man with whom I could share myself. I have been miserable to date and all I ask is that you not break my heart."

Mahoney experienced an irresistible wanting as Judith stepped clear to dip the fork for a sample.

"Judith?"

"Spaghetti is finally ready!"

He drew her close to him. "Judith?"

She could see it all over his face. "Do you want to postpone dinner a bit?"

"I have this urgency to bathe with you. No funny stuff!"

"You *are* bizarre."

"But it shall not survive my lifetime."

They were in the bathtub when Bosco burst into her bark. The suds from the dish soap rose to chest level, and they were holding hands beneath the surface. The door kicked open and a tall man, unshaven, in a trench coat, pantsless, and wearing red high-top sneakers without socks, stood beneath the naked hallway bulb. He was eating spaghetti from a plate with his hands. A blue knit cap tilted down toward his right eye. It was John Hancock.

"However so humble," he growled, "there ain't no place like home!"

"Does he always speak Scottish?" Mahoney inquired.

"Hush!" Judith was alarmed.

"A wee bit of snatch in the aquarium, eh!" John Hancock began to laugh drunkenly. He flung a handful of spaghetti that struck Mahoney on the shoulder. "If I could but banish me cur-sed eyes for memory's sake, me lovely!"

He reached into his trench coat and brandished Mahoney's .357 magnum.

"Jonathan Hancock, you come to your senses!"

"And what've we here, lad?" Hancock nodded to the revolver. "A menace to our fornication, eh!" And then, abruptly, he took aim for Judith. He squeezed until his face burned red, but the safety clip had locked the trigger in place.

"What hath foiled me purpose this time!"

Hancock squinted at the revolver and Mahoney heaved the Lifebuoy from the suds. The family-size bar struck the assailant where it counts and he sank to his knees. Mahoney lunged from the tub and grappled for the revolver. A shot exploded and plaster cascaded from the ceiling.

"Ascend, O deathly chariot!" Hancock bellowed, and Mahoney knew he was entwined in the arms of a madman.

Judith, meanwhile, covered Hancock's head with a towel and tried to discourage his rage by strangulation. The pistol fired again—this time through the bathtub—and water flooded the floor. The phone commenced ringing and suddenly John Hancock was irrepressible. He rose to his feet, shucking Mahoney, and with the towel shrouding his face, emptied the chamber four times without killing anyone. Then, just as suddenly as he had arrived, he was gone.

Mahoney phoned the police and screamed his fucking head off until they promised surveillance through the night.

Bosco was a nervous wreck beneath the kitchen table.

**D A Y**

In the morning edition everyone in town read all about LOVE
TRIANGLE VIOLENCE on page 3. Mahoney requisitioned a new
pistol through Chaney, who hinted that the mayor would more
than likely have the humane officer's vocational ass by day's
end. Mahoney wasn't about to compose an ode to mutability,
and escorted Judith to The Cafe. He made sure she placed two
round rocks in her woolen tote bag, and then scrutinized her
surveillance. The man certainly wasn't taking his eyes off her,
and Mahoney wondered about whom he should worry most.

"Be careful, I love you," Mahoney said, and Judith's eyes
made an inference he hadn't foreseen.

"Not of me, Judith." He had a girl friend again and thanked
his lucky stars. The last thing he wanted to do was let go of her
hand, but this was the beginning, not the end, so he bucked up
and stood in his own two shoes.

"A month from now," Judith said, "we shall more than likely
be perfect strangers."

"But we will be together," Mahoney said, "and maybe someday we'll discover an essential thing or two about the other."

The laundromat supervisor didn't know whom to blame for the
twenty-five drowned cats she found in the twenty-five washing
machines. Mahoney tried a word with God in the van, but by
noon he found himself thinking about the drug that would best

facilitate his removal from the vale of tears. He drove to The Cafe and Phyllis poured a splash of coffee into his cup of bourbon. Judith was waitressing to allow the boy with coiffed hair to practice his omelet technique. The patio was full of sun and Judith was raising the red umbrellas.

"Where's your surveillance?"

"I sent him away."

"Judith?"

"He was staring so horribly!"

"My entire life depends on you!"

"I refuse to live in fear of that man."

"That man is armed with a Smith and Wesson .357 magnum military revolver."

"That remarkable man lived with me for one year."

"That remarkable man is a pernicious drunk!"

"Oh quack, quack, quack, Mahoney."

Mahoney bowed his head. "Judith?"

"The people in the corner are signaling me."

"If something were to happen to you I couldn't go on, okay?"

"You'd get over it."

"I would not."

"You would have to. You would have no choice."

"I am going to pick you up after work."

"I am playing catch after work."

"You're what?"

"I'm playing catch after work with Phyllis. Softball practice begins next week."

Mahoney reminded Judith Chapters that John Hancock had fired six shots into his bathroom fixtures the previous evening.

"Maybe I should leave town," she whispered, and clutched Mahoney's hand. "Will you leave with me?"

"Of course."

Judith didn't believe it.

"When it happens to you," Mahoney explained, "well, it just happens to you."

Judith was wearing a collarless beige shirt, and the unbuttoned V exposed her freckled chest. The rest of her was a maroon apron to her knees, and when she turned around, her abbreviated shorts seemed all the more skimpy. Mahoney wondered why those clogs clacked with increasing sexiness whenever she took one more step away from him into the world. She turned to him momentarily and said, "Keep the faith, dear."

Howdy Doody had a new hairdo; his part had switched sides and the cut was shorter to cover the obtrusive bald patches. The TV, however, exposed the two sides of his born-again mouth. One minute he was mandating the creation of an independent presidential commission to study the nation's future commitment to nuclear energy and the next, right after the soap commercial, proclaiming that *"it is not possible to abandon nuclear power in the foreseeable future."*

Mahoney wondered if there was anything to our weary lives but a burdensome past and a future of accelerating ghoulishness —because the halflife alone of plutonium made the lifetimes between Adam and Eve's and Mahoney and Judith's seem little more than one brief spree of purposeless begetting.

In any case, Mahoney had quite a ways to go before catching up with Edward, The Last Stop's most venerable drunk, and he got started. Nikki walked in the door and Mahoney marveled at the change. She was dressed for court in a suit and high heels and carried a briefcase. Edward said, "Who stepped in it, goddamnit!" There was only Olive and Mahoney and Nikki, and sure enough, it was adhered to the heel of Mahoney's right boot. "Come in here without checkin' first!" Edward shook his head and muttered, "Hippy dippy shitheel!"

Mahoney left his shoes and socks out-of-doors as he'd been

taught to do as a boy. He was pleased no one in his family could see what it had come to, all that wasted training. Nikki and Olive sat at a table beneath the skylight. Olive had made a green silk blouse for Nikki and the two were hugging each other. Edward shouted, *"Beer!"* and muttered something scandalous at the image of the President on the TV.

"Just who is Edward?" Mahoney asked.

Olive was on her feet for the beer. "Harold's daddy."

"The *minister*?"

"The minister's Harold's step-daddy."

Olive served the unhappy father a beer and returned to the table. Nikki looked at her with the eyes of the eternally devoted.

"We tried to reach you all day yesterday," Nikki said.

"Busy," said Mahoney.

"We wanted them two leftover 714s from that groupie fling."

Mahoney just stared at his drink and wondered where in hell relief was hiding.

"The boy Wayno found had some extras, so it wasn't important," Nikki said.

"Our Wayno found someone at the Any Cock'll Do, did he?" Mahoney said.

Nikki fondled Olive's hand. "The important thing is everyone is happy now."

They both laughed. Mahoney reflected on the way Nixon and Agnew had made them laugh at the news conferences. Disgrace comes from above, he realized, only to be recapitulated here, by the small-town anonymous, in these sunless dens of nutritional suicide.

"This young boy," Nikki resumed, "gave us 'ludes. Then we took a walk. A long exhausting walk in the Magic Forest."

"On Rorers?"

"That's why it was so exhaustin', prince. Ah don't believe we got more'n sixty yards from the car."

"Is there a point to this?" Mahoney looked at them through

the bottom of his empty glass. The two women were distended and grotesque.

"Point bein', stinko, that we don't need you for lovin'."

"We fucked in a pine grove," Nikki said.

"And it was much better than with you around," Olive said. "This time ah had someone to talk to afterwards."

"It really was delicious," Nikki confirmed.

"Nobody either runnin' off or fallin' asleep on me." Olive turned and called to Edward, "You gotta git. Ah'm closin' up for lunch."

Edward took the long way out, from wall to wall, but made it safely outside. He glanced both ways as if to cross the street, then sat down on the door stoop.

"Where shall we go?" Nikki asked.

"Ah want one of them Jewish cream cheese and olive sand-wiches with chips," Olive said.

For his part, Mahoney looked out the storefront window showing the street. It looked like a long run. Nikki turned to him.

"You should probably know that Olive and I are leaving for the West Coast next week. I'm relinquishing my staff position and have awarded Wayno the twins. Olive and I are in love. It's the only thing that seems to matter to us."

Olive addressed Mahoney from point-blank range: "Nikki showed me that you gave me orgasms that made me sad 'stead of happy, alone 'stead of together."

"Sooner or later," Nikki said, "to give yourself half a chance of making it these days, you have to renounce your past. We'll probably never see you again in our lifetimes."

Mahoney nodded at both of them and walked out the door to his shoes. Olive shouted after him: "You're just a doggy catcher with a filthy mind and heart."

Then the two women waved to him by moving their fingers separately, as if playing a duet on the piano.

• • •

Outside of town a fox had gotten into Widow Zwillman's hen-house and Mahoney was completing the damage form in the van. Without the sun it was cold enough for his hood, and the widow said he looked silly in a hood with so much hair. She smelled old, like that unused room of Mahoney's brother's, who, along with fifty thousand others, never made it home from the police skirmish that aspired to peace with honor and achieved neither. It must have been the widow's dress that smelled like Tom's curtains. Mahoney was in tears, damning memory, when Chaney broadcast on the CB an all-points for a man in a trench coat last seen fleeing a shooting at The Cafe restaurant.

There were four tables of witnesses. A man in a trench coat—pantless, wearing red high-top sneakers and, over his head, a Supp-hose stocking with an opening for his left eye—stepped from the bushes and walked through two beds of tulips. Approaching the waitress in the maroon apron, he pulled a gun from his pocket and, when the waitress turned her back and began to walk away, said, "You can stop right there, bitch."

Reportedly the waitress kept on walking. The perpetrator fell to his knees and, employing both hands, fired six shots. The man then walked two blocks to the county jail, where he surrendered to the desk officer, Lionel James Chaney.

When Mahoney arrived at The Cafe, a large crowd was jamming the sidewalk. He stood beneath a tree heavy with swelling buds and watched a red light revolving on the roof of an ambulance that pulled away amid an escort of screaming police car sirens.

On the concrete patio, where the blood pooled in a swale, Mahoney could see the outline of the victim in blue chalk. And he knew that what the policeman was scrubbing from the windows once belonged to Judith Chapters.

He ran as only the terrified can run; mechanically, tirelessly. It was a long way to the hospital, frequently more than a lifetime away, but Mahoney knew he must find Judith Chapters waiting safely there for him. Death, which meant never sharing with her again, which meant she was further from his touch than a rock or a neon sign announcing BEER—this was surely impermissible. Surely this world was different from, say, Hell, where redemption and mercy, where a second chance and a single grain of hope, were strictly forbidden. For a woman in white, a nurse, for instance, to say to a creature with a heart, "I'm so sorry, but Judith Chapters was dead on arrival"—this must be impermissible. God would not permit it. This world was not Hell.

Mahoney slammed open the hospital's pneumatic door.

"Judith Chapters," the nurse told him, "is in critical condition with multiple facial and body wounds. She is receiving emergency surgery and there will be no other report available until seven P.M."

NIGHT

Mahoney foundered in time and space and confessed he didn't know how to pray. Then it came to him at once in a reflex as natural as a blinking eyelid and he was all supplication in someone's small yard with birds weltering in a stone bath. He couldn't get the word "lifetime" out of his prayer. He conceded he'd been a fiend and a reprobate in his lifetime, too attracted to dissolution and the proscribed, but only so that he might learn the meaning of goodness beyond history. Surely their lives —each of their little lives—must continue outside of time once they'd learned their lessons here, within time. Judith and he surely came together in time for a reason, and surely time could not erase that reason. What was time compared to love?

Mahoney needed assurances, but God wasn't there. Mahoney knew why, and the tears brought back his breath. He phoned Phyllis's apartment. She picked up on the first ring. Mahoney couldn't stop the tears.

"Judith is alive!"

"She cannot be alive. I saw him shoot her in the head."

"She is in critical condition. She is alive!"

*"Judith cannot be alive, I saw her brains just come right out!"*

Mahoney depressed the metallic lever with his nose. The receiver was still at his ear, and after the company gobbled his dime, the wires whispered *Om* to Mahoney's bowed head.

He was the only one in the hospital waiting room. It was seven o'clock, and America's favorite anchorman reported that a new congressional study reported that 90 percent of all cancers were induced by chemicals introduced to our environment through food additives, insecticides, artificial fertilizers, industrial chemicals, and radiation. Twenty-five percent of all Americans could expect to contract some form of cancer in their lifetime; 5 percent could expect to die of it.

The nurse stepped into the room and touched his shoulder. She was a sudden presence of white within the cigarette smoke, and Mahoney's eyes implored her to spare Judith Chapters.

"I'm sorry to keep you waiting," she said. "Judith Chapters expired at six-seventeen. Members of her family have arranged funeral . . ."

Outside, Mahoney knew there was only poisonous darkness, even though he couldn't sense it. Elaine whispered, "How about when you love someone who's still alive and you know you'll never see him again for your entire lifetime?"

He sat in the van, windows closed, and shut his eyes. When he opened them again it would be yesterday and Judith would be naming flowers in the woods, or it would be four years ago when, through the restaurant window, he first observed Elaine eating an avocado in her white pants and pink blouse. It would be sometime at least in the past, with a better lifetime to come, and his future—this thing that somehow kept happening to him —would have to wait forever for him to choose it into being.

But this was all impossible. Mahoney knew it. He was part of time. She was held away from him forever.

# ENTRAPPED
## AND
## ABANDONED

1. There is nothing we can do, Felice.

We are well into the fall. We have been officially condemned and tomorrow the State shall remove us. It is raining. We are each alone in our six separate houses. The branches of the six maple trees that line the block are barren. Leaves have been down for weeks. The leaves are yellow. They rot silently in the puddles of the dirt road that was once smooth macadam.

The bulldozers can be seen clearly. They are yellow as yellow maple leaves. They are motionless in their stations to the east and west of our block, on the far sides of the two roadblocks of white wooden fencing that will isolate us to the very end. Orange hexagonal signs have been bolted to each of the fences and read:

BLOCK CONDEMNED
ROAD CLOSED

2. Discounting you, Felice, who have left me,

there are twenty-four of us who live on this block of six houses. The houses are old. They are each painted a different color. The Shaws' house is red. The Meekers' is orange. The house I rent, along with the sheriff and nurse, both of whom live above me, is yellow. The house to the west, where the lawyer, the bachelor, the music student, and the seminarian live, with their husbands or wives or paramours, is green. The Reconstruction Home for the Retarded is blue. Then there is Solomon's Market. It is violet.

Do you remember these things, Felice?

Of the two vegetable gardens on the block, one of course is mine. The other belongs to my neighbor, Arthur Meeker. He is eighty-one and can no longer stand erect. He hunches about in a crippled primatial manner.

Three gray squirrels live in the six barren maple trees that bound the road. At the base of each tree, circumscribing the large trunks, a broad white line indicates their imminent demise.

There are eleven automobiles on our block, thirteen televisions, two gas-powered lawn mowers, seventeen electric radios, ninety-two chairs, twenty-three sofas, twenty-eight beds, eleven refrigerators, forty-nine lamps, thirty-one pieces of carpeting, nineteen dressing bureaus, seventeen garbage cans, and innumerable other items I was unable to catalog during the past week. It has all been removed in five white moving vans, which, until an hour ago, were parked in the church lot across the road. Now their absence fills space, Felice.

3. I remember you and I

met at the café three winters ago. Snow was falling softly and Robert Ominios, the retard, introduced us. You were serving him coffee.

He said, "Dis my teaker!" and gazed apprehensively at you through the thick lenses of his glasses. "He learn me," he said, "to read da 'igh 'kool diplomate zo I be neck mayor!"

Two years later, Felice, I sat too closely to another woman, a blonde with green eyes, at a party. The next morning, one of us—which one, Felice?—became contentious.

"Then you admit to wanting to sleep with her?" you said.

"Of course I wanted to."

"But you didn't!"

"I came home with you, Felice."

"Then you are a coward," you said. "You live a lie."

"But of course I am a liar and a coward, Felice. What do you expect from a civilized person?"

"Honesty," you screamed. "Honesty and love."

"We can only aspire to such things, Felice, not live them."

Ominios and I stepped into the café later that day, and you were holding the hand of a man seated at the counter.

"What your wive doing wit' dat man?" Ominios inquired of me.

"Felice is not my wife," I told him.

"Wha'?" He, too, was in shock, Felice. "You mean you live in zin?"

"You are goddamned right, Ominios."

"Chrizt zend you do Hell for dat!"

I told him: "I believe she is holding hands with that man."

He leaned across the table toward me, Felice, and dandruff fell from his eyebrows into his coffee. There were veins in his nose. He glanced over his shoulder at you and turned back to me. "You know wha' I do wid my wive?" he whispered. "I dake 'er do da pound. Day break 'er neck for me!"

"Let us not be misogynistic, Mr. Ominios." These were my precise words, Felice.

"Wha' da'?" he said. "Like V.D.?"

That evening I asked you about the man in the café. We were in the yard picking cabbages from the garden.

"What man?" you asked coyly.

"The man with the mirror sunglasses who was holding your hand."

"Oh," you said, pausing. "He's got a thing for me." You took my hands in both of yours; they were soiled hands. "But you have such tiny hands," you said. "The hands of a neurasthenic. I always wanted a man with big hands."

I withdrew from you, Felice. The darkness had settled early and we were well into the fall.

"You needn't worry, though," you called after me. "I told him I'm living with someone."

I turned to you and said: "What *are* you talking about, Felice?"

"We're attracted to each other but have decided not to sleep together. For *civilization's* sake."


4. Relationships bring to fruition the worst

in all of us. Consider, Felice, the law student and his wife, Lynch and Iris Service. They have lived next door, in the green house, for the past two years. They were married, incidentally, four months ago. This past summer I overheard them talking on their second-floor veranda, which, you might recall, is just above the living room window. I was alone, smoking. It was night and a light burned above them. Lynch Service was immured in a law text. His wife, Iris, dressed in a pink negligee, was sipping wine.

"Give me a kiss," she told Lynch.

They embraced, Felice, with hot, open mouths.

"Are you almost finished!" Iris asked breathlessly.

Lynch Service glanced at the law text and then at his watch.

"Another hour," he said.

"When you're finished," Iris offered, "I'll rub your balls—*if* you shower first and water the plants."


5. Perhaps you wonder

what my life is like without you?

At present, I am seated in the front room before my favorite window. The room is white and empty, with the exception of this dusty refrigerator-and-freezer Safety Brochure that must have fallen behind the sofa you once reupholstered. Do you remember our freezer, Felice?

> *A child trusts you to protect him from entrapment in an abandoned or stored refrigerator or freezer. The entrapment story is simple. To a child, the abandoned refrigerator or freezer becomes a hiding place, a playhouse, in which to lock up playmates. A child does not anticipate the danger. He doesn't even know what suffocation means. But you do! This booklet shows you how to make your unit safe. The procedures are simple. If you follow them, the story can be different—you may save a child's life!*

6. Prior to my engagement to you, I never once felt

abandoned in time or entrapped in space. Still, after my first meeting with your parents—who live along the Cancer Alley of New Jersey, and who, let's face it, were never intended to be mine —my mind could not exorcise a persistent intimation of death. It began, to be honest with you, in your living room on a Sunday in spring. Your entire family had assembled to toast us. Your uncle Shifty, the dentist, stood in the center of the room. He was drunk and burst into an old high school football cheer. Everyone joined in. Do you remember, Felice (this is the truth, isn't it?), the way they intoned:

> A Riky Ko-wax Ko-wax Ko-wax
> A Riky Ko-wax Ko-wax
> A wikity stikity flikity dax
> What's the *shtick* with our running backs!

You and I cast horrified glances at each other (or did we simply smile politely?) and excused ourselves. Uncle Izzy approached and shook my hand. "Congratulations," he said. "Why the hell should you be happy!"

Outside, as I recall, it was humid and gray. Planes descended loudly into Newark International. We had walked one homogeneous block when death took my hand. I averted my eyes whenever you addressed me, and that night in bed I found myself staring wide-eyed at the ceiling.

"What's the matter?" you asked.

"Nothing."

"Do you love me?"

Love, Felice? Well, I suppose, after all, it is necessary to mystify our rather ordinary need for alliances. Then again, how can we be expected to leave well enough alone when the world is dissipating within us at the speed of so many discrete and desperate heartbeats? I'm afraid it is time that divides us. I mean, what comes of counting our little blessings when even they evolve so paradoxically that what was once upon a time a blessing is later a curse?

7. Your mother, Elsie Savings,

at least during the times that I met her, chain-smoked low tar and nicotine cigarettes and spoke in a husky voice while breathing noisily through her mouth. One summer day, I walked with her in the woods surrounding your summer cottage. It was early morning and the tops of the trees smoked with mist.

"Felice tells me," she said, "that the two of you are living together."

"That's right," I confirmed.

She exhaled gray smoke from her nose and studied me directly.

"For what reasons have you decided upon this?"

"We feel happiest when together," I said simply.

"This so-called togetherness," she said, "precludes separate apartments?"

"Two apartments seem unnecessary to us."

"What happens if you argue?"

"We don't argue," I said. "I am not the argumentative type."

"How long have you known Felice?"

"Two months."

"No one argues during the first two months, Taplinger. You are very naïve."

"Possibly."

"And just what does Felice plan on doing in that little town? Because she absolutely promised us after she graduated last January that she'd waitress for no more than four months— until her lease expired. Has she told you she could begin a career in the city, where we have contacts?"

"I'm not certain what she'll do," I said.

"You mean you haven't any plans?"

"We both have jobs and a place to live. That's all I can tell you."

"What sort of job? Felice tried to explain, but I didn't understand a word."

"I teach adult illiterates in the basement of a grammar school," I said, "for which the State pays me forty-eight hundred dollars a year."

"You call that a job for a man no longer single?"

"I'm still very much single, Mrs. Savings."

"How can *you* ruin my daughter's career like this!" she exploded.

I didn't answer her, Felice. I kicked a rock into the pines.

"How old are you, Taplinger?"

"Twenty-five, Mrs. Savings. How old are you?"

"Haven't you any ambition?"

I closed my eyes and smiled. Simultaneously, it seems, we both slowed our pace and halted. Then we turned around and headed back.

"How long do you plan on living together in this tentative manner?"

"I have no idea, Mrs. Savings."

"Do you believe," she asked, staring straight ahead, "that in order to make life bearable we must subordinate self-interest to collective harmony?"

"I believe, Mrs. Savings, that wills war with other wills."

Your mother, Felice, exhaled smoke through her nose with a sigh.

"Your entire generation," she said, "has made a virtue of selfishness. Not one of you seems to realize that convention was established not from groundless fear or ignorance, but to protect us from our own most selfish impulses. That's all I have to say to you."

We reached the clearing of the summer house, Felice, and sunlight came at once. Across the wide expanse of wild flowers and tall grass, I could see you and your father returning from the dock. You had been sailing. The boat was moored securely and you were both walking toward us, holding hands. You both waved in concert, like one will.

8. Lynch and Iris Service leaned over
                          the fence *I* painted, Felice, to invite you and me to dinner. You and I, Felice! It's as strange a combination now as Brooklyn and Dodgers. I accepted the invitation, explaining, of course, that you and I had parted ways and that you would not be in attendance.

"But I thought you were engaged," Iris said.

"We were," I said.

"Did she have a ring?"

"We never did agree on the ring, Iris."

"I'm not sure I understand."

"Felice wanted a ring, but I didn't believe in it."

"And so she didn't get one?"

Lynch glanced at Iris and then smiled uncomfortably at me.

"That's right," I said.

"I don't understand," Iris said. "What exactly in hell is the point of an engagement if there's no ring?"

Lynch lowered his eyes when I turned in appeal to him. I never have been able to answer that question, have I, Felice?

Only Lynch was present when I arrived for dinner. I did not smell food cooking and Lynch seemed embarrassed, standing stiffly in the center of the room, his hands moving nervously in his pockets.

"I'm awfully sorry about this," he said, "but Iris has come down with a headache and cramps. Would you mind if I took you out for a meal?"

We went to Flannagan's, Felice. Lynch drank three quick beers. Night fell and the conversation turned to my breakup with you.

"I can't believe it!" Lynch's laugh implied admiration, even envy, Felice. "How the hell did you do it, for Christ's sake? How long were you with her, anyway? Two years? Three? It's absolutely incredible. You don't mind me going on about it, I hope."

"I don't mind," I said, though I explained that it wasn't I who left you, Felice, but rather you, given my refusal to marry, who decided to leave me.

"Still," Lynch said, "still and all, you laid down the terms. You took command."

"I made my feelings known," I said laconically.

"Unbelievable!"

A waitress deposited two salads before us and Lynch watched her walk away.

"Didn't you love Iris when you married her?" I asked.

He laughed, Felice.

"Me love Iris? Christ no, I didn't love her. I didn't even like her. I think I might have hated her. Still do! But what can you do about it?"

"Why'd you marry her?" I asked him.

"Why'd I marry her? Guilt! Guilt is why I married her."

"I don't understand."

"Oh, come on, Taplinger!"

"You married someone you didn't love. Why?"

"I told you," he said hotly. "I didn't have a choice."

I escorted Lynch Service home after his seventh beer and prepared a pot of coffee for him in the kitchen. Iris emerged from the bedroom in a bathrobe.

"You've gotten Lyn roaring drunk!" she cried. And slamming the door behind me, Felice, she quoted you: "Selfish bastard!"

9. I suppose I was a selfish bastard,

though I'd insert "petty" between "selfish" and "bastard" to do me full justice.

"Must you always leave my books open and face down like this," I said harshly to you one afternoon, spilling over with temper. "Don't you realize you'll break the binding that way?"

"I'm sorry," you said, lowering your eyes nervously.

"These books," I persisted, "are my prize possessions."

"It's the first time I've left one open," you said.

"Actually, Felice," I said, "it is the last time in a long series of unmentioned times you've left one open."

"I'll buy my own copy of the fucking book, then," you said.

"Good!"

"Fuck you!"

"You always do have to have the last word, don't you, Felice."

"On the contrary, Taplinger!"

On another occasion, I said:

"Why can't you throw the can away after feeding the dog? Why must I always clean up after you?"

"I was in a rush this morning."

"It only takes a second, Felice."

"It's no big deal."

"Then why can't you throw it away?"

"I usually do, for God's sake."

"And I suppose," I said, "you usually throw away the Q-tips you use to put mascara below your eyes?"

"Look," you said, "don't nag me just because you hate working with retarded illiterates!"

I remember the time you said:

"I think we should visit our families next weekend."

"I'll think about it," I said, glancing up from the paper. It was raining and I was trying to lose myself in the baseball standings.

"When can you tell me for sure?" you persisted.

"Let's not arrange anything formally," I said.

"I never see my parents anymore," you complained. "It's absurd."

"So go see them!" I snapped, crumbling the paper. "Do you need me to take you there? We have separate cars. You can visit whenever you want. Why blame me?"

"Because it would be *nice* if we did some things together," you said.

"But why? Didn't God incarnate us in separate bodies so that we might be independent as well as lonely as hell?"

"I find your tone of voice destructive."

"I find your request suffocating and a pain in the ass."

"I find it odious you'd rather be by yourself than with me."

"Why the hell can't you respect my need for privacy?"

"For the same reason you can't respect my need for company."

"Move out, then!"

"You're a selfish bastard, Taplinger!"

"You're a rope around my neck, Felice."

10. Do you remember our last day
together, Felice? I had
written your parents a letter canceling the engagement. We
were on our way to dinner. A thunderstorm was racing in from
the west. The trees lashed about wildly and you were hurrying
three steps ahead of me while trying to discuss something.

"If you want to speak with me," I said irately, "don't walk
ahead of me."

"I'm not," you called back.

"What the hell do you mean you're not," I said. "Are you
or are you not walking ahead of me?"

You stopped and allowed me to draw even with you.

"No," you said.

"No?" I said hatefully. "Then I submit we speak a different
language."

"Undoubtedly."

"Undoubtedly," I fumed, "you either walk in front of me or
behind me. On the few miraculous occasions you do walk even
with me, you are constantly bumping into me. Two years together and we haven't even learned to walk."

"I was walking ahead because I'm scared of thunder," you
said softly.

"Then why the hell didn't you say that? All you had to do
was ask me to hurry up."

"But why must *you* always walk so morosely behind? Why
must *you* always dawdle along in some private reverie?"

"It just so happens I enjoy watching thunderstorms, Felice."

"Oh really," you said caustically. "I thought you only enjoyed disparaging me."

That afternoon, in the worst rainstorm of the summer, with
downtown flooded, you stomped across the little city and
located an efficiency apartment for yourself.

II. Perhaps you wonder about:
   a. Our landlord,

who is still a drunkard? The rent still keeps his cup runnething over. Last week I saw him walking through the season's first snowstorm in an unironed blue suit, the pants of which were torn and too short and revealed brown bruises on his ankles. His sneakers were black high tops and he wore a soiled fedora. He was unshaven and cradled a brown box in his arms. In the middle of the box, like a sacred icon, Felice, stood a bottle of whiskey.

He halted and stood before my window of vision. Raising his eyes to the trees, he cried: "Get in the goddamn house! Get in the goddamn house!" I still do not know, Felice, where he lives nor what else he does besides walk drunkenly round town or sit drunkenly in the park in the sun. Naturally, the first of each month he is sober enough to collect the rent. This is all I know of him. And one more thing: from the appearance of his suit I infer that he, too, lives alone, without love. It seems he shall be just one forever.

   b. Curtis Brown, the deputy sheriff,

who lives upstairs?

Once, while smoking marijuana on his veranda last spring, we observed women passing below on the sidewalk. He volunteered that he had never before slept with a black woman. I confessed to the same disappointment. He said: "Sheriff always sayin' to me, 'Come on now, Curtis, tell the truf. What is it like with a colored piece?' And Curtis always tellin' the man, 'Damned if I know, ain't never done one up!' "

I do not doubt, Felice, that Curtis was telling the sheriff the truth about his sexual preference. Curtis's former wife, who still frequently pounds upstairs to scream about alimony payments, is, you'll recall, a large white woman with plati-

num hair and a badly matched glass eye. His present com-
panion, whom you never met, is a frail white woman with
buckteeth whose armpits tend to perspire and stain her
blouses. She, too, frequently screams at Curtis Brown. Her
voice issues shrilly down the radiator column. "You don't
love *me*," I will hear her cry late at night. "You love *it*!" And
Curtis Brown will rejoin: "And you loves me for *it*, too,
lady!"

c. Mrs. Shaw, who is scared

of animals? She came bursting
through the door last March in a blaze of snow. I was lying
in the living room drinking a hot toddy and watching snow-
flakes accumulate on the windowsill. You were gone, Felice,
and it was afternoon. She slammed the door behind her and
leaned breathlessly against it. Her eyes were closed. I called
attention to myself by clearing my throat. She cried out and
frantically lit a cigarette.

"I didn't mean to frighten you," I said softly. "I'm sorry."

Her hands were blue with cold and visibly trembling.

"It is I who am sorry," she whispered emphatically. "I am
so terribly ashamed of myself."

She is a small woman, Felice. Standing before the door in
her boots and red winter hat, she seemed a child with the face
of an old woman. To her right, through the icy window of
my living room, I spotted the nurse's Great Dane peering
into the house. His nose breathed steam that melted the ice
crystals on the windowpane.

"It's a phobia," Mrs. Shaw whispered shamefully, retreat-
ing from the window. "It's the curse of my life."

"You're safe now," I assured her. Safe with me, Felice!

I heard the nurse calling the Great Dane from the side
door of the apartment and then I heard them both noisily

climbing the stairs to the apartment above ours. Mrs. Shaw's horrified eyes lifted to the ceiling.

"Would you like me to walk you home?" I offered.

But Mrs. Shaw no longer seemed cognizant of me. She dropped her cigarette to the wooden floor and extinguished it roughly with her foot.

"I'll thank you not to breathe a word of this, young man!" She spoke severely, and then was gone, hurrying down the front steps.

But what's the point of keeping secrets, right, Felice?

When I retrieved her cigarette stub from the floor and examined it closely, it turned out to be the same brand you and your mother used to smoke.

d. Mrs. Yesining, one of the retarded

illiterates, whom I began to teach just before you left town?

She still wishes to save her child from the Child Protection Bureau, which claims her six-month-old son was covered with serious skull and back bruises, and which consequently confiscated the infant. Mrs. Yesining is learning to read in order to enhance her chances of regaining custody of her son. What did we do, Felice, to enhance our chances? I'm afraid we tried to incorporate our lives into something the State calls FAMILY. Mrs. Yesining's little family has gone to hell, too, Felice. Her husband, Harrison, suffered a stroke last summer and sits paralyzed in the State's psychiatric ward. So Mrs. Yesining is now alone, still an epileptic with a hearing problem, a sobering case of halitosis, and an inadequate set of false teeth that has deformed her mouth so that her speech is slurred to near incoherence. Surely there is no way out for her, Felice. She, too, is entrapped and abandoned, but she can't even read our little Safety Brochure.

Last week she just up and ran. She mailed me a postcard that read:

I am sumware new. A fiend
Rite this 4 me. I hapy like
U now. Buy! Buy! Mrs. Yesining.

e. Robert Ominios, whom we used

to invite in for brownies and milk?

He still passes the window each day, though now he is accompanied by three or four other residents from the Reconstruction Home who collect the neighborhood newspaper and glass and drag it along in red wooden wagons to the scrap plant at the edge of town for money. Last year, Felice, the Home used the money to acquire a pool table, and this fall they decided upon a used black-and-white TV. Now, Robert Ominios is as fond of TV as he once was of, well, your tits. He stares at and reflects upon the screen with the same nervous and vacant wonderment he once reserved only for you. When I first informed him that you and I had decided to separate, he said: "My wive leave me doo. Dat why I redard now."

This past summer, Felice, Ominios phoned to explain he was laid up in the county hospital. His leg was to be amputated.

"Where are you exactly, Robert?"

"I in dah ho'pital."

"Which hospital? Where?"

"Da blue one!"

The man is forty-one, Felice, and he began to weep inconsolably.

"You my teaker," he gasped. "You 'uppozed do be here. Dell dem no. 'Old my 'and."

I visited him, Felice, but I did not hold his hand. He had

been admitted to the hospital, I learned, because of a case of pleurisy related to a diabetic condition. The operation did not entail the amputation of his leg but, rather, the removal of specific blood vessels close to the surface of his thigh.

He was lying rigidly in bed when I first saw him. His eyes seemed terrified behind his thick glasses. He needed a shave and his hair was thin with large portions of his scalp completely bald, as if he suffered from mange.

"I gonna die," he whispered melodramatically.

"Of course you're not going to die," I told him.

"Da doctor dol' me."

"The doctor told me you'd be fine," I lied.

"I dell you da zdory of my live," he said. "Af'er I die I be famiz."

Listen to this, Felice:

"Ad fivdeen I ztard workin' for Bol'en Bruderz Bak'ry. Den I 'ad a paper roude. I waz fivdeen zdill. Den I zdarded pickin' beanz at Hal'dead Comp'ny. Den I work at a cannin' facd'ry. Den I work for a guy name Zlim. He dead now. He waz a good bozz. I watched ditchez and cook. Af'er dat I work for a fitch-fry plaze on Green Zdreed. Den I work for Diger'z Diner on Park Zdreed, watchin' ditchez. Den I got fired and wend do work for Al Beg'o for zevendeen yearz az a ditchwatcher and glean-up man.

"I got married and Al Beg'o fire me. I dell Al Beg'o, 'Up your azz!' I work ad Larry Marley'z junkyard. I god fired and wend do Flor'da. I work a garbadz druck for five yearz. One night I gum back do de drailer and my wive gone. Den I dravel aroun'. Den my wive come back and we dake a vacazun do Drendon, New Jerzey. I work in a zigar fac'dry wid my wive. Den I god a job ad a rubber fac'dry wid Ralph, a color guy. He drew a barrel on my 'ead and I 'ave an operazun. Den my wive leave me again, zo I dook 'er do da pound an' dey broke her neck. Den I god redard. Now I gonna die."

12. I cannot explain why

affection dies between us, Felice. Certainly it doesn't ask our permission. It ends by independent laws, as the life of leaves ends, or as a straight line infinitely extended ends in a circle, back where it started, closed in upon itself. There is apparently no way of preventing low tide. We must move inevitably through the world, like a stick racing along a stream.

No, Felice, I never did have faith in very much, though, technically, I was faithful to you. There never was anyone else. Naturally, I confess to my share of fantasies, for we must all believe that if there is a way in, there is a way out. I'm not talking about transcendence here so much as a hiding place, a little spicy surcease, a bandage for the growing leaks of the heart. You will never find me in white, Felice, and I am not interested in saving grace. If there is something beneath our underdeveloped lives of ice, it is too far away, too inaccessible and demanding for me. I'm afraid most of us still find sensation too seductive to worry about redeeming our selves' histories of lost causes. I'm afraid we want our lives this way, Felice.

13. I did not see you

for a week after you moved out. I sat alone late at night with the window open. Boys would pass the window, shouting and throwing rocks at street lamps; cats would fight. Ofttimes I would be awakened in the chair by the newsboy delivering the paper at dawn.

One morning I wandered sleepily to your apartment and climbed the empty trellis to your window. I peered inside. You were asleep on a mattress in the center of the floor. Beside you, to your right, lay a naked man, wearing mirror sunglasses and athletic socks. I turned away and wandered aimlessly home.

The following day, as I was hitching up the hill, you stopped to pick me up. It was raining, Felice, and you were smoking a cigarette. I stared straight ahead, watching the windshield wipers.

"How are you?" you asked.

"Don't you believe," I said, "that a failed relationship warrants a period of mourning?"

"I mourned our relationship for the last six months we lived together."

"Have you nothing more masochistically interesting to do than allow yourself to be violated by some delinquent who wears socks to bed?"

I give you credit, Felice, you flushed.

"I wasn't violated at all. I enjoyed myself immeasurably."

"Have you no interior dimension," I said. "Must your revenge be so transparent? Must everything be purely aesthetic in nature for you to appreciate it?"

"How else am I supposed to nurture a relationship?" you screamed.

" 'The specific character of despair,' " I reminded you, " 'is precisely that it is unconscious of being despair.' "

You pulled the car onto the shoulder of the road. Lightning flashed once, and then the rain came in a heavy, violent cascade.

"Get out," you commanded.

"It's raining," I said. "I have a cold."

"Get out!"

"If I get out, you'll never see me again."

*"Get out!"*

14. I suppose it is true. There is nothing

we can each do but fall with a little class. Though we certainly didn't. Of course, we did not know that when the preacher sayeth from dust to dust, he imagined circles within circles. We interpreted till death do us part a bit too literally, I'm afraid.

Some time ago, I observed my neighbors congregating at the end of the block. They gathered for the candlelight vigil protesting our eviction. Due to the cold rain and wind, however, Mr. Solomon—do you remember him, Felice, the grocer with the brand on his left arm?—had distributed waterproof sparklers to each of the participants. So instead of a funeral march of dim candles, the walk along the block suggested a parade of renewed hope. I did not move from my chair before the window. The reflection of my face floated translucently in the glass pane before me, and within my reflection, as if in my mind alone, walked the members of the block. Above them, a light shone through the stained glass of the church vestry so that the image of Christ nailed to the cross floated above them as if it were part of the black sky, a constellation to which we could each only raise our eyes in wonder.

It was then, Felice, that someone fell. The crowd closed in upon itself and my neighbors knelt down in the rain. Curtis Brown splashed across the street, toward the house, and pounded up the steps. I met him in the hallway.

"What's happened?"

"Ol' man Meeker done kicked the can, man!"

I tried to help, Felice, but there was nothing to do but keep umbrellas over Arthur Meeker and his sobbing wife until the ambulance arrived. Curtis Brown had phoned the county sheriff, the city police and the emergency squad, so the street, beyond the CONDEMNED sign, was ablaze with crimson flashing lights. Curtis stood with the enforcement people in his gray deputy sheriff cap and raincoat, and Arthur Meeker lay covered in mud. He had fallen forward, Felice, face first, into the street. The impact of the fall had broken his glasses and partially loosened his dentures, which made him appear to be smiling sideways. His eyes were open and covered with mud. Undoubtedly, he had died first, then fallen.

15. We are only as decent,

Felice, as our limited capacity for decency allows. So I have constructed a trap for the mice that eat the paprika and shit on the silverware. The trap is a small rectangular contraption of two chambers with aluminum doors at the terminal sides that drop suddenly whenever one of the floor plates is touched. I have corralled six brown mice in two hours and have transferred them to a shoe box that once belonged to you. I have placed molded cheese in the box, but whenever I peek through the holes in the cover, I notice that the mice are huddled together in a single corner, anxiously, as my poor neighbors seemed anxiously huddled around the corpse of Arthur Meeker.

Fear is everywhere, Felice. Pain seems so willing to accommodate all forms of life. I think few of us will ever fear and tremble as visibly as the steer at the moment of slaughter, but still, how is this commensurable to our surviving the perfect horror of that Sunday afternoon just after the finch rose from the feeder?

We are each seeds, Felice. These six mice that remain for the night in the shoe box are seeds. And so is this form that lay naked beneath three blankets in this darkness in this abandoned apartment. I am a seed. Even your apparition, Felice, floats before me like a long white silky seed blown in the wind.

In time, by laws of nature—by gravity—all seeds bolt to new seeds. And in time, Felice, they all go bitter. Consider, for example, the lettuce we planted that final summer. Or point to a life that hasn't—gone bitter, I mean. You can only prune a flower so many times before new flowers will refuse to appear. I'm afraid people can go to seed with one another only so many times, Felice, before it all goes bad.

You said: "How am I supposed to meet someone if I don't sleep with them?"

"I refuse to even answer that," I said.

"Would you have come to dinner over and over if we hadn't slept together?" you asked.

"What kind of question is that?" I said.

"So you thought I was indecent for sleeping with you that first night you took me for a drink?"

"The difference was," I said, "that I knew things were workable between us."

*"You consider this horrible end workable!"*

"Nothing ends, Felice, it only changes."

"Just fuck off, Taplinger!"

16. I remember the day

you left town, Felice. You passed me in the road in your red car. I waved and stopped you. I stood before the open window. You were smoking a cigarette. There was no protection in your eyes.

"I'd like to speak with you," I said.

"I'm leaving town," you said.

"When you get back, then."

"I'm leaving for good," you said.

You offered me your hand and I took it. You turned your eyes away after one final moment of appeal. My throat closed as if the air were miasmal.

"I'll write," you said.

My last glimpse of you was of your hand as it reached out the window to flick ashes into the wind.

17. So now there is nothing left

to do but withdraw from here. These rooms were never ours anyway, Felice. We *paid* to live here. Objectively, without our little trinkets filling the place, I can see that the rooms are cold and loveless. It is an old and unclean place. I should have known better. Your mother and father were against it from the start and you felt it cost too much to heat. It was wrong. But soon enough there will be nothing left, no tangible sign, neither proof nor landmark, that we were ever here together. In six months, by spring, people will drive through the space that was once the major boundary of our lives. The State will remove every brick and nail and beam of wood. No trace will remain. There will be nothing to point to. The foundation of our happiest and most intimate moments will be as far under as Arthur Meeker, though there will be no skeleton to prove it was more than a mistaken memory. Perhaps the world works to our advantage.

18. Let me tell you
of the future, Felice. I will stand across the road with my neighbors and watch it all tumble down. Officials of the State will blow whistles and wear yellow helmets and metal-toed shoes. Their large hands will frighten Mrs. Shaw's mother-in-law. The mice will thump their feet in the shoe box in the cold fall air. The bulldozers will then invade the street and roar toward the large crane, on which will be suspended the rusted metal sphere that is as large and frightening as a dead planet. The crane will swing the metal sphere no more than ten times before Solomon's Market will be a sad pile of violet splinters.

We will watch the destruction until the dust forces us to retreat to the western edge of the block, whence the wind will be issuing. Officials with chainsaws will commence to fell the maple trees, and Robert Ominios will be standing beside me, clutching a little red wagon and blinking his eyes vacantly behind his thick lenses.

"It ain'd ober," he will tell me ardently. "I luze my room. I luze my friendz. Bud I no gry. You my teaker. You learn me 'igh 'kool diplomazy. You make me mayor. I ged dem do rebuild deze houzez. I god 'ope!"

Robert Ominios will then step before us, Felice, still holding the wagon, and he will announce:

"Doe'n' gry! We gan do id! My wive leave me bud I do good. I be good mayor to you peoplez. You zee. It ain'd ober. Geep 'opin'! Pleaze!"

In the distance, high in the air, far above the church steeple and the roar of the chainsaws in the bare spaces where the maple limbs once supported the sky, I will spot a long series of geese in expansive chevrons, beating south, toward the sun that now and then will attempt, unsuccessfully, to burn through the clouds. It will be late into the fall for these geese to be so far north, Felice, and each time the scream of the chainsaws abates for a moment, the calling of the geese will grow loud and wild with urgency.

Ominios will stand with his back to me to follow the flight of the geese. Both arms will stretch into the air; his small jacket will ride up on his body. His legs will be short and heavy, and in his excitement over the migration he will step into a puddle that will be ankle deep. But once the geese have disappeared into the horizon, he will become abject, bowing his head to the puddle in which he will be standing. When he turns to me, his imbecile eyes will be tearful behind his glasses.

"I god no plaze do go in dis worl'!" he will sob.

And I shall say: "Faith overcomes the world, Robert."

This is the extent of my life without you, Felice.

# ABOUT THE AUTHOR

Born in 1951, SCOTT SOMMER was raised in New Jersey and educated at Ohio Wesleyan and Cornell universities. He has received a National Endowment for the Arts grant and a Creative Artists Public Service fellowship. His first novel, *Nearing's Grace,* was published in 1979. Mr. Sommer lives in New York City.